TEXAS
SICARIO

OTHER TITLES BY HARRY HUNSICKER

Arlo Baines Thrillers

The Devil's Country

The Jon Cantrell Thrillers

The Contractors
Shadow Boys
The Grid

Lee Henry Oswald Mysteries

Still River
The Next Time You Die
Crosshairs

TEXAS SICARIO

HARRY HUNSICKER

THOMAS & MERCER

Text copyright © 2019 by Harry Hunsicker
All rights reserved.

Published by Thomas & Mercer, Seattle

www.apub.com

Amazon, the Amazon logo, and Thomas & Mercer are trademarks of Amazon.com, Inc., or its affiliates.

ISBN-13: 9781503905412
ISBN-10: 1503905411

Cover design by Ray Lundgren

Printed in the United States of America

To Alison

- EL EMPRENDEDOR -

(The Entrepreneur)

Alejandro Sandoval liked money.

Occasionally, the thought crossed his mind that this might be a sin.

If he still attended mass, he might have asked his priest. But he had little time for church, or for much of anything for that matter, his second job being more labor intensive than he'd imagined. And more lucrative.

Alejandro tried not to think about sin and priests and such.

Instead, he concentrated on the good fortune that had come his way, the opportunity for a better life for his family and him.

After all, wasn't that what America was all about? The chance to better yourself?

Right now, there was so much plastic-wrapped good fortune in the back room of his tire store that he couldn't process the numbers in his head, the dollar figure that belonged to him from each shoebox-size package.

His cut was only a tiny fraction, but the quantity this week alone was so vast that he wondered what he would do with the extra cash.

Fortunately, this was the last of it for a day or so. A few dozen kilos stacked in a cramped area behind the office, the air thick with the chemical tang of new tires and a fragrant herbal aroma from the packages themselves.

The man from the restaurant—another spoke in this particular wheel of opportunity—would arrive at any moment to take the shipment to a place where the distribution would begin, an area of the operation with which Alejandro didn't concern himself.

Alejandro's life was full enough without worrying about others' responsibilities. The businesses, a wife and two sons, the ever-increasing amounts of cash that needed to be handled.

A life so different from that of his father, who'd spent decades as a cobbler in Guanajuato, hunched over the shoes of rich men.

Alejandro wondered what Papa would make of his only son. Surely this newfound success would change the old man's stubborn way of thinking. These people with their packages were just businessmen, just like Alejandro himself.

His phone chimed. A text from the restaurant man, now in the alley behind the tire store.

Alejandro replied that he was ready.

Twenty minutes later, the transfer was complete, the restaurant man departing in his van.

Tomorrow, one of the *jefes* would drop by Alejandro's tire store with a grocery sack full of cash and information about the upcoming schedule.

Until then, Alejandro was free to relax. He lit a cigarette, his only indulgence, and gathered up the trash that had accumulated in the storeroom over the past few days.

Outside, the sky was cloudless, the heat fierce. August in Texas, so much hotter than the mountains back home.

He walked across the alley, threw the trash into the dumpster.

That's when the man in black appeared, and Alejandro Sandoval came to understand that for every opportunity, a price must be paid.

The man wore a clown mask, a silencer-equipped pistol in one hand.

Alejandro started to speak, but the words wouldn't form, his tongue thick and dry.

The man raised his arm, and Alejandro felt a thump in his belly.

He shuddered. An instant later, he lay on the dirty asphalt, gasping for breath.

Pain spiked deep in his stomach. The taste of blood filled his mouth.

The man pointed the pistol at his face.

"Please, don't." Alejandro's voice was a whisper, lungs not functioning quite right.

The killer didn't reply.

"*Por favor, amigo.* My wife, my children, they need me." Alejandro tried to move his legs, but they refused to work properly.

The killer shook his head. *"No soy tu amigo."*

"Tengo dinero," Alejandro said. "Much money. All for you. Just don't shoot again."

Silence.

Alejandro realized he was going to die in a few moments, passing on to the next life from this grimy spot in the alley behind his place of business. No sum of money could save him.

Without warning, the killer fired again, a bullet smashing into Alejandro's knee.

The pain was blinding, but he had no strength to cry out.

The killer's mask shifted like he was smiling.

He aimed at Alejandro's forehead, and the world turned black.

- CHAPTER ONE -

Days like this, when the whiskey got the better of him, Javier liked to talk about death.

"These are dangerous times," he'd say. "Evil is at the gate, and we shall all die soon if we are not vigilant."

I liked to point out that we didn't have a gate, aiming for a bit of levity, but I never got much of a response. Javier's sense of humor was—oh, how should I put it?—askew, so he didn't appreciate jokes all that much.

He had suffered more than I had. He'd watched his family die, a wife and two daughters, cut down by gunfire on the streets of his hometown, Nuevo Laredo. Because of that, I was pretty lenient when it came to his missing sense of humor and discussions about evil and death and whatnot.

On this day, when the topic came up, we were in a bar called El Corazón Roto, the Broken Heart, sitting in a booth at the front.

It was a few minutes before noon, and he had just started on his second glass of Jack Daniel's, on the rocks. I was nursing a cup of coffee.

"You feel it, too, yes?" He took a sip of his drink.

"Feel what?"

"The hairs on the back of my neck. Bad things are headed our way."

"Maybe you have a rash," I said.

Javier's neck was always telling him some disaster was about to hit.

"Why are you and I even friends?" He rolled his eyes. "This is what I get for discussing such things with a gringo."

"You got any other friends? Gringo or otherwise?"

He waved a hand dismissively and stared into his glass.

I knew he was thinking about the girls, María Elena and Gabriela, who would have been twelve and thirteen this year.

Thirteen years old, the same age as my son if he'd lived.

I pushed away those thoughts, drank some more coffee.

El Corazón Roto catered to working-class Latinos, an increasingly large customer base in Dallas. The place was small and out of proportion, a long, narrow room with high ceilings, like a casket. The walls were decorated with neon signs advertising Carta Blanca and Modelo. A pool table was in the back by a jukebox loaded with conjunto music, Mexican rap, and Marty Robbins, the last one a favor for me, to be played only when there wasn't a crowd.

"You are armed today?" He rattled the ice in his glass.

"*Sí.* I have my *pistola.*" A small-frame Glock he insisted I carry, tucked inside my waistband, like when I used to work undercover.

Javier owned El Corazón Roto and the *mercado* in the much larger building attached to the bar. I was head of security, which had little to do with actually keeping things secure. Mostly, I took care of him when he'd had too much to drink, which wasn't all that often, and commiserated about the travails of the small businessman, usually a daily occurrence. A patrol service made sure the businesses were safe.

This early on a Thursday, we were the only ones in the place other than the bartender.

In a few hours, the men would show up, dusty and sweaty from building this or landscaping that, and the room would fill with the sound of glasses clinking and people speaking Spanish.

I finished my coffee as the front door opened, and a shaft of light cut through the gloom.

A moment later, a man appeared, short and squat, his hair close-cropped.

He blinked several times and sauntered to the bar. His skin was dark brown, the color of coffee beans, stretched over wide cheekbones, the face of a Mayan warrior.

He took a seat at the far end of the bar, maybe thirty feet away, out of earshot.

"You know him?" Javier asked.

I shook my head.

"Look at his clothes," he said.

I had already noticed the black jeans, matching western-style shirt, and the boots with the silver toe tips. Not the usual wardrobe of an El Corazón Roto customer.

"Let it go," I said.

"You know the rule. No narcos."

Javier had a thing about people in the drug business, his family having been killed in the crossfire between two competing cartels.

I sighed. We'd been over this before. The smuggling operations along the Rio Grande didn't have a significant presence in North Texas. The police and the courts in this part of the world weren't as corruptible as farther south, the journalists not as easily coerced.

"Those clothes don't mean he's a narco," I said.

"Look at his wrist. What about that?"

I turned toward the bar. The man wore what appeared to be a diamond-encrusted watch. I didn't reply.

"What do I pay you for?" Javier said. "Earn your keep."

"You haven't actually paid me in a while."

He stared at me, face blank, brown eyes unblinking. He was in his early forties, a little younger than I, but looked ten years older.

Our relationship wasn't based on money. We were close because of the suffering we'd endured but rarely talked about, the daggerlike pain that never quite went away, grief from losing all that we had loved.

I slid out of the booth.

The man with the fancy boots watched me approach. He'd ordered a Bud Light and took a drink as I handed my cup to the bartender.

"Cómo estás?" I said to the stranger.

"Coffee?" He pointed to the mug as the bartender emptied the dregs.

"I'm not much of a drinker."

He took another sip of beer. "Your friend handles that for the both of you, huh?"

I pulled a cocktail napkin from the stack by the beer taps, wiped up a small spill while the bartender rinsed out my cup, studiously ignoring both of us.

"Where are you from?" I asked.

"You have a nice place here. Business good?"

He was observant, noticing Javier's whiskey, and forthright, asking about business. The hairs on the back of *my* neck were starting to take notice, and the ex-cop in me wondered what game he was playing.

The bartender frowned, leaned close to a monitor next to the cash register.

"We work hard at keeping it nice," I said. "Me and the owner."

"I'm from South Texas." He adjusted his watch. The diamonds sparkled in the neon light. "So, what's a white guy doing in a place like this?"

"Everybody has to be somewhere."

"Señor Baines." The bartender called my name, pointed to the screen. "You should see this."

The monitor, visible to anyone standing at the bar, was connected to a series of video feeds. The one in the middle displayed the parking lot directly in front of the entrance to El Corazón Roto.

The lot was huge, much bigger than what was needed for a relatively small bar. Most of the spaces would be filled over the weekend, shoppers at the *mercado*.

At the moment, only a handful of cars was present. In the distance, at the far edge of the property, I could see blue and red lights flashing.

The man with the expensive watch glanced at the monitor. *"La policía."*

"You know anything about that?" I asked.

"Not me, amigo. I'm just passing through." He pushed away his half-finished beer and headed toward the door.

- CHAPTER TWO -

I'd been a cop most of my adult life, up until eighteen months ago, first as a trooper with the Department of Public Safety, then as a Texas Ranger.

Dead bodies were nothing new to me, but that didn't make seeing one any easier, especially when it was somebody I knew.

We weren't exactly close, but Alejandro Sandoval had always seemed like a decent enough guy, a low-end entrepreneur, hustling to get a slice of the American Dream. Certainly not someone who deserved to be gunned down in an alley.

But bad things happened to good people all the time, as any police officer could tell you, and his death was just one of many I'd seen that made no sense.

Alejandro's body lay sprawled in the middle of a rectangle formed by yellow crime scene tape. The tape bracketed an area behind his tire shop and the dumpsters at the rear of Javier's parking lot.

From my vantage point by one of the dumpsters, it appeared that he had been shot at least three times: in the head, abdomen, and knee.

A coroner's assistant stood in the shade of a hackberry tree, fiddling with his phone, his van parked nearby. Inside the crime scene tape were several forensic investigators armed with clipboards and digital cameras, a half dozen uniformed officers, and a homicide investigator I knew named Sam Ross.

Javier stood by my side, staring at the body, swaying on his feet a little. Ross nodded hello but continued working.

It was twenty minutes past noon, the temperature pushing ninety-five. The air smelled like garbage—grease and rotting food, sour milk.

"Go inside," I said. "They'll be here awhile."

Javier shook his head. "You should find that *puta* with the fancy watch."

I'd already used my phone for a quick scan of the video from the camera system.

Alejandro's body had been found to the north of El Corazón Roto, maybe two hundred yards from the entrance. The man we'd seen in the bar had come from the east and departed in that same direction. None of the other cameras showed where he'd gone—not too surprising, since there were gaps in the coverage.

Also, the camera facing north barely captured the police cars, showing only the flashing lights. The lens wasn't powerful enough to pick up individuals at that range, as the homeless people who sometimes hung around the dumpsters seemed to intuitively know.

I'd explained all that to Javier, plus the fact that it didn't make very much sense for the killer to stop for a beer at the place next door while waiting for the police to arrive.

He didn't care. To him, the guy with the silver-toed boots didn't belong in this neighborhood. Therefore, he was a suspect.

Javier called out to the coroner. "Why don't you cover him up?"

The coroner's assistant glanced up from his phone but didn't reply. A moment later, he returned to his screen.

"Hey." Javier raised his voice. "I'm talking to you."

The coroner looked up again, an exasperated expression on his face.

"His family," Javier said. "They shouldn't see him like that."

The coroner rolled his shoulders and got in the van, turning on the engine.

"They can't cover him yet," I said. "Might contaminate the scene."

I'd once worked a case in a little town outside of Corsicana; a waitress in a honky-tonk had been stabbed to death in the men's restroom, her body dumped in the metal trough that served as a urinal. Forensics had taken nearly ten hours processing the scene, bagging and tagging DNA samples, old cigarette butts, the odd used condom.

Ross stepped around a tech taking pictures and approached us.

"Arlo Baines," he said. "Last I heard, you'd left town."

I shrugged. "Now I'm back."

After my family had been killed, I'd spent the better part of a year drifting. At the time, motion seemed to be the only thing that came close to filling the hole in my heart. In the end, I learned that nothing could patch that empty space, so I returned to the place where I'd spent a large part of my life.

Sam Ross was wearing brown Sansabelt slacks and a yellow short-sleeve dress shirt. He was in his midfifties, so white he probably got a sunburn from the TV.

Javier stared at the homicide detective with open contempt, his eyes like slits, lips twisted into a frown. A fan of *la policía* he was not.

"What are you doing here?" Ross made a great show of looking in either direction. "You live in *this* neighborhood?"

Alejandro's tire store was located in the southwest portion of the county, between Cockrell Hill, a small incorporated area completely surrounded by the city of Dallas, and a neighborhood called Oak Cliff.

A hundred years ago, the area had been full of middle-class whites. Then the population had transitioned to black. Now, this section of town was dominated by first-generation immigrants, overwhelmingly

Mexican with the occasional Central American family thrown in just to mess with the census people.

I started to answer, but Javier cut me off.

"Alejandro." He jabbed a finger at the body. "You need to put a sheet over him or something."

Ross fanned himself with his clipboard. "Hot as balls out here, and I got somebody telling me how to do my job."

"His wife usually brings him lunch about now," I said. "I'd hate for her to see him like that."

Ross shook his head wearily. He asked one of the crime scene guys if he was finished. The tech shrugged and then nodded, indicating he'd done the absolute minimum and wouldn't be doing anything else. A couple of minutes later, a white sheet covered Alejandro Sandoval's body.

I caught Javier's eye, pointed to the bar. "Go inside. I'll be there in a few minutes."

He glared at the police officers and then staggered away. When he was out of earshot, I relayed to Ross the information about the video system and the man with the expensive watch. He wrote everything down and then gave me the preliminary time of death, between ten and eleven, at least an hour before the man in black had wandered into the bar, which was about the same time that one of Alejandro's employees discovered his body and called 911.

"Any video from the tire store?" I asked.

He shook his head. "One camera on the front. Doesn't show anything useful."

"How big of a team do you have canvassing the area?" I didn't see many uniformed officers, just the ones inside the tape and a couple of others by the store itself. Certainly nobody who appeared to be combing the other businesses on Alejandro's street, asking if they'd seen anything.

"You stop reading the papers? Between the pension mess and the budget cuts, manpower at the DPD is fifteen percent below where it should be."

"So no door-to-door?" I tried not to sound frustrated. "This is a homicide, you know, not jaywalking."

"Did I say that?" He fanned himself again. "The sheriff's department's been pitching in until we get fully funded. Some trainees from the academy are gonna be doing a canvass. Hopefully in a few hours."

"Trainees?" I said. "In a few hours?"

"It's a dead Mexican, Arlo. Give me a blonde girl from a good part of town, and I can put more uniforms on the street."

I wondered if it was time to get a better camera system for the *mercado* and the bar.

Ross pointed behind me. "Who's your little buddy?"

I turned and saw Miguel, a street kid Javier and I looked after.

He was an orphan, eleven years old, and the last person on earth I wanted to see what was going on in this particular alley.

- CHAPTER THREE -

Javier and I had found Miguel in a bus station restroom three months earlier. He'd been huddled in the corner by a condom vending machine, eating the remains of a Big Mac he'd pulled from the trash, while a man in a raincoat told him what a pretty boy he was.

The man appeared to be fondling himself, which didn't sit well with either Javier or me.

So, while Javier hustled the youngster out of the restroom, I throat-punched Mr. Raincoat and threw him into a stall, headfirst.

The boy was filthy—hair matted, face caked with dirt—and skinny, clothes hanging off his body like they were a size or three too large. Javier spoke to him in Spanish and English, asked his name, about his parents, where he was from.

The boy just stared back, his eyes big and round, face blank. He had no reaction until a police officer walked by. Then he hid behind Javier and tried to make himself small, arms pressed to his sides, shoulders hunched, gaze following the uniformed man.

After the cop had passed, I knelt so we were eye to eye. *"Tienes miedo de la policía?"* Are you scared of the police?

He looked at Javier and then at me, lips pressed tightly together as if he were afraid to let the words out. After a moment, he nodded.

A few yards away, the officer entered the men's room, where Mr. Raincoat was no doubt pulling his head out of the toilet at that very moment.

"Tienes familia?" Javier said. "Do you have family? Or anyone?"

The child's expression was all the answer I needed.

I stood, took his hand. *"Vámonos."*

He seemed to understand we weren't a threat. He grasped Javier's hand as well and walked outside with us on either side. We headed to Javier's pickup, threading our way through the homeless people and passengers waiting for their buses.

"No one is going to hurt you," I said.

He nodded again like he understood English and climbed into the cab, sitting in the middle. Javier drove to Target and went inside to buy the boy some clothes, leaving me in the truck. While he was in the store, the boy looked at me and said, *"Me llamo Miguel."*

"Hi, Miguel. My name is Arlo." I held out my hand.

He hesitated, then shook, smiling for just an instant. Then he fell asleep on my shoulder, almost in a coma, a slumber so deep that he didn't awaken even when I carried him from the truck.

We fed him and cleaned him up. Since I was living in a motel, Javier made a place for him at his house, the bedroom that his girls had shared.

Over the next few days, I contacted several individuals at the Department of Public Safety and CPS, asking if anyone had reported a missing boy who fit his description. At the same time, Javier reached out to some people on the border, trying to find out what he could about the child, if anything.

At no point did we consider turning him over to the authorities. The odds were high that he was undocumented, and neither of us wanted him to be deported or get lost in the Kafkaesque machinery of foster care. The child had obviously been through enough already.

The days turned to weeks, and we all settled into a routine. Javier looked after the boy in the morning and evening, and I, along with several trusted employees of Javier's, took the afternoon shift.

Miguel slowly grasped that we represented stability, and though he never spoke willingly about his past, gradually we pieced together his backstory.

He was from Piedras Negras, just across from Eagle Pass.

He had no siblings, a sister having died in infancy. His parents had been killed in a car crash several months before he ended up in the Dallas bus station. An uncle had brought him across the border, and the story became murky after that.

Something about the police and a shoot-out. The uncle was wounded, and he left Miguel on the doorstep of a business associate, a person who sounded like a low-level smuggler running a whorehouse on the side. Or a pornographer. It was hard to tell.

Miguel wouldn't or couldn't say what had happened from that point until we'd found him by chance, after dropping off Javier's cousin so she could catch a bus back to Laredo.

No matter. He was a good kid, and I enjoyed his company, a bittersweet reminder of what I had lost.

Now the boy was staring at the sheet-covered body of a man he knew, and I imagined his past was crashing in on the sliver of normalcy we'd tried to provide the last few months.

"What is going on?" he asked. His English had improved, but he still spoke haltingly, with a thick accent.

I moved to block his view. "Let's go inside."

"Dónde está el Señor Sandoval?" He craned his neck to see around me.

I decided to tell him the truth. "He's dead. *Muerto.* Someone killed him."

The boy stared at the sheet-covered corpse, face blank.

A squad car screeched to a stop by the perimeter of the taped enclosure, and two uniformed officers exited. One ducked under the tape. The other stood by the car and spoke into his radio.

Miguel grabbed my hand. His skin felt cold, and his teeth chattered, like he'd been swimming in ice water.

"You OK?" I asked. *"Estás enfermo?"*

He tugged at my arm, a worried look on his face. *"Por favor.* We must leave."

- CHAPTER FOUR -

Javier's main business was the Aztec Bazaar, sort of a flea market / low-end shopping mall catering to Hispanics.

The Aztec Bazaar was housed in an old discount store, a 150,000-square-foot box that had been subdivided into individual stalls, too many for me to keep track of, most no larger than the guest bedroom in a starter home.

The bazaar was more than just a shopping facility, however. It was a gathering place for Spanish speakers, a social hub for working-class people whose roots lay south of the Rio Grande.

On weekends, some families would spend most of the day there, buying clothes, browsing for furniture, getting a haircut, seeing the dentist, or just visiting with each other at one of the half dozen food kiosks and restaurants scattered throughout the building.

There wasn't much you couldn't get at the Aztec Bazaar. Used televisions and new tires, cowboy boots, piñatas, toys, jewelry, tools and hardware, religious statues, *quinceañera* gowns, cell phones, small farm animals . . . the list went on.

Miguel and I headed for the main entrance, around the corner of the building from El Corazón Roto.

The entryway contained a shrine to Our Lady of Guadalupe, a five-foot-tall plaster statue, her green robes highlighted by lemon-yellow shards of sunlight silhouetting her from behind. Dozens of candles and flower bouquets lay at her feet, offerings from the patrons of the Aztec Bazaar, requests for the blessed virgin's intercession in various business issues, personal matters, and affairs of the heart.

Beyond the entryway lay the market itself, row after row after row of stalls, a maze that probably made sense to Javier but was utterly incomprehensible to me. The mix was a jumble, nail salons and auto parts stores next to each other, a chiropractor across from a tattoo parlor.

Once inside, I looked at my watch. It was well past lunch. Time for a growing boy to eat.

I turned to Miguel. "Should we have tacos?"

He smiled. "Tacos. *Sí.*"

I waited for him to choose. There were many options for this particular category.

Miguel headed to the right, down a narrow passageway. Midway down the hall was a taqueria that had recently opened, a place that Miguel particularly liked.

The Aztec Bazaar was beginning to fill up, the start of the weekend crowd that would culminate on Sunday afternoon when the walkways became clogged with shoppers, throngs of people shoulder to shoulder like Times Square on New Year's Eve.

A few minutes later, we were eating at a small table across from a three-chair beauty parlor owned by a woman named Maria.

Maria was in her late thirties, single and childless, her husband having died in Afghanistan the year before. More often than not when she saw Miguel and me together, she would sit with us, occasionally asking us to dinner at her house. I could feel the loneliness coming off her in waves, so I kept my distance.

Beyond a few hookups with random women I'd met in equally random bars, awkward couplings I usually regretted immediately, I hadn't been close to anybody since my wife had died.

Maria was a nice person, attractive and pleasant to be around, so I often wondered why I didn't let her cook me dinner. I was lonely, too. Some days were worse than others, but the emptiness was a constant companion.

Grief was a funny thing, never far from your mind but hidden, a serpent slithering unseen through the dark places of your heart, making you wary of entanglements.

As we ate, I looked at Miguel and said, "Have you ever seen a dead body before?"

No answer. He stared at his plate, munching on a fajita taco.

"Mr. Sandoval," I said. "He was a nice man."

Silence.

"It's OK to be sad that he's dead."

Miguel stopped eating. "Where is Maria?"

Good question. If she wasn't busy, she usually sat with us.

I shifted my chair to one side in order to get a better view inside the salon.

There were no customers visible. After a moment, I saw her in one of the styling chairs, staring at the people walking by. When our eyes met, she stood and moved out of my view.

"Es una mujer buena," he said.

I nodded in agreement. She *was* a good woman. One who for some reason didn't feel like visiting with us today.

"Señor Sandoval." Miguel pushed away his plate. "He was *malo*."

I stopped eating. "What do you mean?"

No answer.

"Miguel. Do you know something about Señor Sandoval that I don't?"

21

The boy had always been an enigma, even after settling in with Javier.

He was prone to periods of silence, not talking at all for hours on end.

Sometimes he repeated phrases that were gibberish, others that were obscene.

He was deathly afraid of a homeless person I occasionally gave food to, a slightly deranged woman in her sixties who always dressed in a ragged skirt and blazer, business attire for a job that no longer existed, and liked to shout at pigeons and people who got too close. (To be fair, the homeless woman had yelled at Miguel on several occasions, though I was pretty sure he'd had worse done to him before he came to be with us.)

I had often wondered how much of his condition was due to the trauma of losing his parents and the subsequent time spent in the company of some very bad people and how much was inherent in his makeup. Did he fall somewhere on the autism spectrum?

He didn't reply.

Before I could press him, my phone rang. I answered.

Javier was on the other end. "The narco is back."

- CHAPTER FIVE -

The man with the silver-toed boots was at Restaurante Consuelo, sitting at a four-top. The restaurant, located at the rear of the bazaar, was really just a glorified food stand that served enchiladas and burritos. The place had only a few tables, all of them set out in a wide spot in the walkway. He was the lone customer.

The man was drinking another Bud Light, an empty plate with a wadded-up paper napkin in front of him.

Javier stood across the hall in the doorway of a tax preparer's office, maybe twenty yards away. He didn't look wobbly anymore. He looked alert and sober. I took up position next to him.

The man in the silver-toed boots glanced across the walkway and raised his beer in my direction, toasting my arrival.

"*Pendejo,*" Javier said. "Would you look at him?"

"What am I looking at? He's just sitting there."

Javier jerked his head in my direction and glared at me. "I want him gone. Now."

"He's not doing anything."

"After what happened, you say that?"

"He didn't kill Sandoval."

"How do you know?"

OK, that was a valid point. I didn't know for sure. All I had to go on was my instinct, honed after twenty-plus years as a cop.

Something was off about the man; that much was clear. He didn't belong at the Aztec Bazaar, eating lunch, shopping for nail guns and chrome wheels. He was working some angle, which nine times out of ten proved to be illegal. But I didn't believe that he killed Sandoval. That smelled like a professional hit, and a professional would not stick around to sample Consuelo's enchiladas.

Nonetheless, I decided it was time to learn what I could about the man and then urge him to move along. I ambled across the hall and sat down at his table, uninvited.

He took a sip of beer. "You want some coffee? Or is it time for you to start drinking?"

"What's your name?"

"Your amigo Javier, he doesn't like me very much, does he?"

I pondered the fact that he had taken the time to learn names. The squeeze had to be coming soon.

"Javier Morales, owner of the Aztec Bazaar." He smoothed back his hair. "He's come a long way from Nuevo Laredo."

"Let's stay on topic. Tell me your name and what you're doing here, and then maybe we can talk about Javier's improbable rags-to-almost-riches story."

"You can call me Fito."

I pulled a notepad from my pocket, jotted the word on a fresh page.

"Why are you writing that down?" He cocked his head. "You're not a cop anymore, are you, Arlo Baines?"

I closed the notepad. "Am I supposed to be impressed that you know my full name and what I used to do for a living?"

The man who called himself Fito didn't reply, a smug look on his face.

"It's almost like you have some magical way of finding out stuff."
I smacked my forehead in mock surprise. "Oh, wait. That's Google."

"You have a sense of humor." He smiled. "I like that."

"What are you doing here, Fito?"

"I'm a, whatdoyoucallit, student of commerce. Businesses, how they run, that sort of thing. Javier, he has himself a good operation here."

So this was a shakedown. Next would come the offer of his services to prevent break-ins, theft, vandalism, or whatever, all for a reasonable weekly fee, payable in cash. If we didn't agree to his terms, well, this was a rough neighborhood, and who knew what might happen.

"I think you should leave now, Fito. That'll be best for everybody."

He stared at me, any pretense of being friendly gone, his eyes cold and flat like a mackerel on ice. After a few moments, he reached into the breast pocket of his shirt and withdrew a crumpled bill, a twenty. He tossed it on the table and then stood.

"How is Miguel doing?" he asked. "You gonna send him to school in the fall?"

That was a sliver of data not available on Google, the existence of the youngster, something Javier and I went to great lengths to keep on the down low.

"A boy who's been through what he has, he needs some structure, you know what I'm saying?" Fito smiled.

My limbs tingled and my mouth got dry as adrenaline shot through my system. To say I was protective of the child was an understatement, like saying the North Pole was kinda chilly at night.

Without standing, I shot my hand out and grabbed the fleshy part of Fito's thumb before he could react. I twisted the thumb out, a simple move that caused a lot of pain. The only way to relieve the pressure was to walk forward . . . into the table. If he tried to extricate himself in any other way, I needed only to apply a little more pressure, and he'd be wearing a cast for the next few weeks.

Fito's eyes went wide, but he didn't resist or make a sound.

"Whatever your play is," I said, "leave the boy out of it."

He stared at me, nostrils flaring with each breath.

I cranked the thumb a millimeter more, just about to the point where bones would start to break.

His face turned red, but he didn't make a sound, lips pressed together tightly.

"What's gonna happen next," I said, "is you'll walk out of here quietly and not come back. *Comprende?*"

He nodded once.

I let go.

He jerked his arm away and staggered backward, cradling the injured hand. He stared at me for a long moment, then nodded slowly, like he had made a decision of some importance. Then he turned and sauntered toward the exit at the rear of the building.

When he was out of sight, Javier dashed over to the table.

"What happened? Why'd you grab his hand?"

I didn't answer. Instead, I went to the counter and asked for a to-go box. A moment later, I returned to the table with a Styrofoam container.

"Did you scare him off?" Javier asked.

"For now. But he'll be back."

"What? How do you know?"

"Because that's the kind of man he is." I used a pen to put the empty beer can in the container, careful not to smudge any fingerprints.

Javier read my face. "Miguel? Is he in danger?"

I didn't answer his question because I didn't want to lie to my friend.

"Let's go check on him just to be safe," I said.

- CHAPTER SIX -

I'd left Miguel in the manager's office, playing a video game, Kiki the receptionist keeping an eye on him.

They were buddies, Miguel and Kiki. She was in her late twenties and had four children, a couple around his age. A warm, mothering type, quick with a joke, she doted on Miguel, who in turn relished the attention.

He was pretty self-sufficient, as eleven-year-olds went, and we all took turns caring for him—Javier and his cousins who lived nearby, the people who worked at the bazaar, and myself.

Javier trotted down the hallway, pushing people out of his way. I followed, the Styrofoam container with Fito's beer can under one arm.

Ninety seconds later, Javier burst through the double doors leading to the offices where the people who ran the Aztec Bazaar worked.

Miguel sat on a sofa in the waiting area, a Game Boy in his hands. Kiki was behind a desk, tapping on a keyboard.

They both stared at us, eyes wide.

Javier scooped up Miguel, hugged him tightly.

The youngster looked at me, eyes full of fear, not understanding what was going on.

"It's OK," I said. "Javier, put the boy down. You're scaring him."

Javier muttered something in Spanish about death and vengeance.

"Everyone is safe," I said. "Let him keep playing his game."

Kiki stood. "What's wrong?"

Javier put the youngster down but kept a hand on his shoulder, obviously not wanting him to get too far away.

I described Fito. "Miguel, have you or Kiki seen this man?"

Miguel shook his head.

I looked at the receptionist. "What about you, Kiki?"

"I don't think so," she said. "Who is he?"

Javier cut his eyes my way, obviously undecided as to how much to reveal.

"A shoplifter," I said. "He's probably gone by now."

Kiki frowned, obviously wanting additional information.

"We're going to take Miguel home," I said. "Señor Javier will be leaving, too."

She looked at me and then at her boss, her expression indicating she didn't believe that a mere shoplifter could get this reaction.

I hustled Javier and the boy away from the office.

Outside, the parking lot was about half-full. It was the middle of the afternoon, and the sun was fierce, the heat like an unseen presence, blanketing everything.

My pickup was in a reserved space next to Javier's, under a small carport near the front entrance.

I hopped in the driver's seat. Miguel and Javier climbed in on the other side.

In the distance, on the far side of the parking lot, I could still see several police cars clustered around the spot where Alejandro Sandoval's body had been found. At least the coroner's van was gone.

Miguel looked at me as I cranked the engine. "This man with the silver on his boots."

I backed out of the parking spot.

"Viene por mí?" Is he coming for me? Miguel sounded frightened.

"I will kill anyone who tries to hurt you." Javier balled his fists, breath coming in heaves.

Miguel whimpered, fidgeting in his seat.

"No one is after you," I said. "That guy was just a troublemaker we ran off." I shot a look at Javier. "That's all."

The boy nodded like he wanted to believe me.

I put the pickup in drive and continued to glare at Javier, trying to send him a telepathic message to lay off the theatrics. We needed to speak in calm, soothing tones and not talk about people getting hurt or killed.

He finally noticed me, but he had no response. His face was blank, eyes half-closed. Something was brewing inside the man, and I hoped it didn't cause him to drink more. He needed to be sober, or relatively so, because I wouldn't be able to help out with Miguel for a while.

I pulled out of the parking lot, headed north on Westmoreland, past tiny wood-framed houses and strip centers occupied by Mexican grocery stores, pawnshops with signs in Spanish. No one spoke.

Javier lived close by, a dozen or so blocks away, in a tidy two-bedroom brick house on Edgefield. The neighborhood, just south of the central business district, was different from the area around the Aztec Bazaar. Javier's block was in the middle of a gentrifying area, an uneasy mix, working-class whites and Latinos giving way to hipsters and gay couples.

I stopped several times in the middle of various blocks, doubled back twice, checking for a tail, before I turned onto Javier's street. I paused two houses away for a full minute, just to make sure we were in the clear, then pulled into his driveway, parking in the carport at the rear.

Javier and his wife had bought the place when they moved to Dallas twenty years ago, before the artisanal coffee shops and organic cheese vendors had started to arrive.

The yard at one point had obviously been a source of pride, beds full of roses, trumpet vines growing on a trellis, a fountain in the middle of the lawn.

Now the land, like the house itself, had fallen into disrepair. A stagnant soup of water and leaves filled the fountain. The lawn was patchy, the flower beds overgrown with weeds, and the trellis had fallen over.

I left Javier and Miguel in the truck while I checked the perimeter.

Nothing was disturbed or out of place. The gate leading to the alley was secure, and the doors and windows of the house were locked.

I returned to my pickup, told them everything was OK. Miguel scampered to the back stoop and waited for Javier to come and unlock the door. When the boy was out of earshot, I told Javier to wait. He stopped and glared at me.

"You planning to drink any more today?" I asked.

He shook his head.

"Order pizza for dinner. Maybe watch some movies or play checkers. Don't talk about death or how we're all in danger or any of that crap."

He stared at me sullenly. After a moment, he nodded.

The neighbor to the north of Javier's house was a white guy who claimed to be in the advertising business but spent most of his time tinkering with a broken-down VW and watching tennis. If Fito came nosing around, I doubted he'd be much help.

To the south lived Torres, an ex-marine in his early sixties. Torres ran four miles a day and was built like a seasoned piece of oak, hard and damn near unbreakable. He served as the unofficial mayor of the block, sitting on his front porch, taking note of everyone who passed by.

I waited until Javier was inside and I heard the deadbolt lock. Then I went next door and found the former marine. I described Fito, asked him to keep an eye on Javier and the boy for the next few hours. He readily agreed.

After that, I drove to the bazaar, stopping first by the dumpsters at the rear of the tire store.

The crime scene tape was still in place, but most of the people investigating the murder of Alejandro Sandoval had left, except for Ross and two uniformed officers.

I got out, the Styrofoam box in one hand. Ross looked like he would rather have his gums scraped than arrange for the beer can to be fingerprinted, but he relented after I said I would owe him a solid. Cops were a lot like mobsters and bankers; they understood the value of having people in their debt.

I left the Styrofoam container with him and then parked in my spot at the bazaar.

It was late afternoon, and I wanted to find out what I could about the man who called himself Fito. It wasn't going to be much fun, but the best way to accomplish that with my limited resources was to talk to people at the *mercado*, a one-man door-to-door.

I planned to start with Maria, asking if she knew anything about the man in the silver-toed boots and also why she'd avoided me earlier. I'd been a cop too long to not trust my gut. And right now, my gut was telling me something was very wrong at the Aztec Bazaar.

- CHAPTER SEVEN -

Maria had gone for the day, her beauty parlor the only establishment on that aisle that was closed.

I asked the people on either side if they knew why she had shut down on what was promising to be a busy evening.

Shrugs for answers—not surprising, since both places were filled with customers and, despite my Spanish skills and close relationship with the owner of the bazaar, I was still a gringo ex-cop.

I went back to the first place on her aisle, a discount electronics store, and asked if anyone there had seen Fito. They didn't think so, but did I want an in-dash nav unit for my car?

And so it went. No one had seen or would admit to seeing the man. An elderly white guy who shined shoes at one of the barbershops remembered seeing someone who sort of looked like Fito, but he couldn't say what day that had been.

Two hours later, I had talked to about half the shop owners at the Aztec Bazaar. I had encountered a woman going into labor; a young man proposing to a girl who looked like she was about fifteen; and a *curandera*, or folk healer, selling her services from a spot by the women's restroom. What I didn't encounter was anybody who knew anything about Fito.

I made sure someone was able to take the pregnant woman to the hospital; gave my best wishes to the newly engaged couple; and ran off the *curandera*, since she wasn't leasing a stall. After that, I debated my next move while I waited for Ross to run the man's fingerprints.

The best play at this point would have been to review the day's security footage from all the cameras, a fairly arduous undertaking best accomplished on something other than a cell phone.

Before climbing that mountain, I decided to visit El Corazón Roto to see if anybody there had seen the man.

It was a little after six in the evening—prime time for the after-work beer-and-a-shot crowd—when I trudged around the outside of the *mercado* and stepped into the bar.

I paused for a moment, letting my eyes adjust to the light, enjoying the feel of cool air rushing over me.

The place was almost full, forty people or more, all of them brown-skinned men. The jukebox was playing one of my Marty Robbins's tunes, "Big Iron on His Hip," a song about an Arizona ranger who kills a notorious outlaw. An odd choice, given the crowd at the moment.

The bartender waved me over.

I threaded my way through the drinkers, ignoring the stares, the gringo interloper invading their space. Work long enough where you're the only white guy, and you get used to that.

The bartender pointed to the rear. "A man's asking about you."

"Who?"

He lowered his voice. *"Policía."*

The crowd of working-class Hispanics had given the booth at the far end of the room a wide berth, like a force field was keeping them away.

As I made my way to the rear, all I could see was a gray Stetson, tilted down, and a gnarled hand holding a bottle of Carta Blanca.

When I reached the booth, the man wearing the Stetson looked up.

"Howdy, Arlo. Been a while, hasn't it?"

His name was Aloysius Throckmorton, a former colleague of mine at the Texas Rangers.

He was Anglo, in his late fifties, part of a demographic that viewed dinner at Applebee's and tickets to the tractor pull as a fine night out with the missus.

He was also the last person in the solar system I expected to see in El Corazón Roto.

Unless he was on the job.

"What the hell are you doing here?" I sat across from him. Aloysius Throckmorton and I had a history together—and not a good one, from my point of view.

"Getting my diversity on." He took a sip of beer. "We're all the same, comes down to it, even me and a bunch of taco humpers."

He thought of himself as wielding a rapier wit. At times, he might have been considered humorous, except for the racism and the fact that he had the charisma of a prison guard.

I didn't say anything, trying to control the anger rising in my gorge.

"You want a beer or something?" He wore the standard getup of a Ranger—the Stetson, of course; a western-style khaki shirt with enough starch in it to stop a bullet; a five-pointed star pinned to the breast pocket.

"No." I shook my head. "I don't want a beer or something."

Age had taken a toll in the year since I'd last seen him. His mustache was grayer, and the flesh under his chin hung a little looser. His complexion was the same, however: skin creased and worn like leather chaps left too long in the sun.

"Thought you would have retired by now," I said. "But here you are, all badged up and ready to go."

"Got a few bales left in the barn. I'll be out to pasture soon enough."

"I'm there already," I said. "But you knew that."

Two years ago, when I was still a Texas Ranger, a group of crooked, drug-addled police officers had murdered my wife and children. The officers had subsequently been killed, their corruption brought to light, but for a short period of time, I was the main suspect in their deaths.

The Ranger assigned to investigate me and determine my fitness for continued duty had been Throckmorton.

He had recommended my termination, despite the fact that I'd been cleared of the murders. I'd quit anyway, two days after burying my wife, son, and daughter. At that point, there didn't seem to be any reason to keep working. Or doing much of anything.

"Couldn't you scrounge up a security gig in a better part of town?" he asked.

He knew my job, which meant he'd done some homework, which meant this wasn't a social call.

"What do you want, Throckmorton?" I kept my voice even.

One thing I'd learned over the years—anger was a choice. Right now, I didn't want the emotion to interfere with the tasks that lay in front of me. So I chose not to dwell on our past interactions.

"Had a little excitement next door, what I hear."

"Ross told you about me, didn't he?"

He stared at his drink for a moment and then nodded. From the seat next to him, he picked up the Styrofoam container I had given to Ross earlier in the day, the one containing Fito's beer can.

"Tell me about this." He put the container on the table to one side.

The jukebox clicked to another Marty Robbins tune, "El Paso," the long version, a five-minute ode to a Mexican bar girl. Some of the crowd looked around, confused, obviously wondering why there weren't any songs *en español* playing. A couple of people turned our way, curiosity giving way to mild irritation.

Throckmorton smiled. "I just love me some Marty Robbins. Don't you?"

When I didn't reply, he looked away and sighed, surveying the room like he was bored.

"How well did you know Alejandro Sandoval, the vic at the tire store?" His tone was casual, somebody making conversation about the weather.

"We were acquaintances. You know anything about what happened to him?"

No answer. He took a drink of beer.

"I need that container back." I held out my hand. "The man whose prints are in there threatened my employer."

He patted the Styrofoam. "I'll run the prints for you."

I shook my head. "Give me the box. You're the last person I want involved."

He smiled, a look that was anything but friendly. "I'm not asking, Arlo. I'm telling."

I rubbed the bridge of my nose, stifled a yawn. It had been a long day.

"You see the bartender?" I asked.

Throckmorton glanced toward the bar. A second later he looked back and nodded.

"A couple of weeks ago, I caught some crackhead trying to jack his pregnant wife in the parking lot. She's four months along. Their first child."

He continued to stare at me, face impassive.

"Anyway, long story short, for the foreseeable future, the crackhead won't be able to use either hand to hold a pipe, and the bartender, well, he feels like he owes me big-time." I paused. "His three brothers who are sitting at the bar feel the same way. You know how the 'taco humpers' are about family."

He glanced away again, jerking his head back like the movement had been involuntary.

I continued. "All it takes is me scratching my nose the right way, and the four of them will turn you inside out. They don't give a damn if you're a Texas Ranger or not."

A long few moments passed.

I wondered if the bartender even had a girlfriend, let alone a wife. He was new, and I didn't know him all that well.

"When did you turn into such a ballbuster?" Throckmorton slid the Styrofoam container from the side of the table to a spot between the two of us.

I pulled the box close to me, resting my hands on top.

"How about we go at this a different way?" he asked. "*May* I run the prints for you? Pretty please."

"Why do you care about whoever last held that beer can?"

"I have a new assignment." He looked across the room again, staring at the bartender. "Liaison between the Texas Department of Public Safety and the DEA."

I remembered Fito's expensive watch and Javier's certainty that he was a narco.

"New initiative out of DC," he said. "The feds are supposed to play nice with the state and local authorities."

"And they picked you. Mr. Congeniality."

"Give me the box, Arlo. That way we don't have to get bogged down in subpoenas and all that malarkey."

I hesitated for a moment and then pushed the box back across the table.

Throckmorton was a stand-up guy, as bigoted assholes went. He'd run the prints and get me an ID on the man with the silver-toed boots, probably quicker than Ross would have.

He tucked the container under his arm and stood by the side of the table. He wore a tooled leather belt and matching holster. He rested one hand on the butt of his pistol.

"One more thing." I described the man who called himself Fito. "I'm not a big believer in coincidences," I said. "Strange that this guy just shows up right after Alejandro at the tire store gets his library card canceled."

"We live in strange times." He adjusted his hat and left.

The crowd grew silent as they watched him go. Then they looked at me, and for the first time since I'd started working for Javier, I felt a slight trill of unease run up my spine.

- CHAPTER EIGHT -

I left the bar, got into my pickup, and headed to my domicile du jour, an extended-stay motel on the other side of downtown near Baylor Hospital.

As I drove, I checked in with Javier, who sounded sober. He said that he and Señor Torres and Miguel were watching a Fast and Furious movie and eating pizza. I told him I would pick them up in the morning and ended the call.

Fifteen minutes later, I parked at the back of the Value Rite Inn, near the stairs leading up to my room, a second-floor unit offering a nice view of a convenience store run by a family of Iraqi refugees and a Vietnamese restaurant.

The neighborhood was a hodgepodge—dive bars and places to sell plasma, new apartments and old houses, used furniture stores, a guy slinging dope in the parking lot of the Burger King—the usual for this section of east Dallas.

I'd been there almost four weeks and would move to another place soon.

The transient lifestyle was not a money issue. I could afford to buy a home or rent an apartment. But since the death of my family, I preferred not to have entanglements, not to set down roots. Movement, or the illusion thereof, was important.

I parked, chirped the locks, and headed to the Vietnamese place, an old IHOP now decorated with lanterns and statues of Buddha.

Maria was sitting at a table by the front window eating an egg roll when I walked in. She motioned for me to join her.

I hesitated for a moment and then sat on the other side of the table, for some reason not all that surprised to see her there even though she lived in a suburb south of the city, a long way from this particular neighborhood.

"Small world," I said.

"The girls in the office, they told me you come here a lot."

I wondered how the girls knew this. Miguel or Javier, perhaps?

"Seemed like the only way we were ever going to have dinner." She smiled.

I smiled back to be polite but didn't speak. Without asking, the waiter brought me a glass of ice water and an order of spring rolls.

"How's Miguel?" Maria asked.

"Fine, all things considered. He's a good kid."

"You have a happy look on your face when you talk about him. That's nice."

I fussed with my napkin, took a drink of water. She did the same, both of us nervous.

"You closed early today," I said.

"I suppose I did, come to think of it."

We sat in silence for a few moments.

"Why don't you ever want to come to my house?" she asked.

"You know about my wife and children, right?"

She nodded. "You know about my husband, don't you? What happened to him in Afghanistan?"

I nodded in return.

The waiter came back to take our order. Maria got the beef with snow peas. I had my usual, a bowl of chicken pho. The waiter left, and it was just the two of us and our dead spouses, a really screwed-up double date.

We gossiped about people at the Aztec Bazaar for a while, then the conversation petered out.

After a few moments, Maria said, "Your wife. When you close your eyes, do you still see her face?"

I looked out the window, unsure how to respond. I wasn't used to talking about my grief. I remembered my wedding day, the taste of the cake, the sun on my shoulders, my wife's dress.

"I used to see my husband, as clear as day. Now, not so much. He's still with me, but there's less of him. Like something that's getting smaller in a rearview mirror."

"Like you're forgetting something you swore you never would," I said.

She nodded.

A betrayal was another way to put it, but one you couldn't control. Worse than the loss itself in some ways.

I didn't want to tell her that my wife's features were slowly disappearing, too. Each day her smile became less distinct, her face blurrier, writing on a piece of paper left out in the rain.

We didn't speak for a while, both staring outside.

The waiter brought our food.

We ate, made small talk. When we were finished, she said, "Who was that man you were asking about today?"

"No one important." I wondered who had told her about my inquiries. "You know anything about him?"

She shook her head.

The waiter slid the check onto the table.

"If I tell you why I closed early, you're going to think I'm nuts." She stared down at her plate.

"Maybe." I smiled. "Try me."

"I had this idea that my husband needed me." She paused. "Like he was calling out for help, but I couldn't get to him."

I remembered the times I'd had the same sensation.

"I drove to the cemetery, just to see his grave." She lifted her chin. "Pretty crazy, huh?"

"The mind's a funny thing." I paid the bill.

She turned to face outside again, and we were silent for a short period of time.

When the waiter brought my change, she said, "You live around here?"

• • •

Five minutes later, we stood at the foot of my bed. We were only a few inches apart, but the gap that divided us felt like a canyon.

She leaned in and kissed me.

I kissed back, enjoying the feel and taste of a woman I hadn't met in a bar, someone I might actually care about at some point. I pulled her close, our bodies pressed together.

A few moments later, we broke apart, each moving away at the same time, like something unseen had come between us, an invisible wedge.

Tears glistened in her eyes.

"Sorry," I said.

"It's not you." She wiped her cheeks. "It's too soon."

We sat on the bed, side by side, staring at the black screen of the television.

After a couple of minutes, she stood, walked to the door. "They say that you like to be on the move."

I shrugged.

"Why'd you stop at the Aztec Bazaar? Why there of all places?"

"Javier, I guess. He and I are friends."

I didn't want to tell her how we met, how a grief-stricken Javier was about to jump from an office tower in downtown, and I stopped him. If I told her any of that, then I would have to think about why I sometimes found myself at that office tower, looking down at the hard, cold pavement below.

"You're a nice man, Arlo. Maybe you should keep traveling."

"Why do you say that?" I wondered if she was referring to what was going on at the bazaar.

"Just an observation. Maybe traveling suits you." She opened the door and left.

I pulled the shades back, watched her get into her car and drive away.

Even though it was early, I went to bed anyway, hoping to dream about my wife, but there was nothing, only the blackness of sleep.

- CHAPTER NINE -

Javier and Miguel reported an uneventful night when I picked them up at nine the next morning. I dropped Javier at the bazaar and then took Miguel to the mall to buy new clothes. The kid was growing like an irradiated weed.

It was a little before eleven when the boy and I pulled in to the parking lot of the Aztec Bazaar for the second time, and I saw a four-door Maserati in my slot next to Javier's pickup. I double-parked behind Javier's Chevy, and—resisting the urge to key the side of the expensive auto—I entered through the front door with Miguel.

The place was teeming with shoppers, promising a very busy weekend.

I walked Miguel to the office, intending to leave him with Kiki the receptionist.

Much as I hated the veiled threats issued by the man who called himself Fito, he did have a point. We needed a long-term plan for the youngster, not just shuffling him around among Javier's employees and family members. A time would come when he'd need to be in school, with kids his own age. Have a semblance of a normal life.

That time would arrive another day, however. For now, I wanted nothing more than to keep him safe, something that I failed to do for my own children.

Kiki was at her desk in the front, head down, tapping on a keyboard.

Across the room, on the worn leather sofa that passed for a waiting area, sat a woman in her forties, slender with dark hair pulled back in a shoulder-length ponytail. She had olive skin and wore a form-fitting, sleeveless dress, peach-colored, the hemline stopping a few inches above her knees. A strand of pearls hung around a neck that could best be described as elegant and shapely. I wondered if she'd made a wrong turn on her way to Neiman's.

She was leafing through an old copy of *People* magazine and looked up. She smiled at Miguel. *"Hola, señor."*

The boy clutched my hand but didn't reply.

"Es un poco tímido," I said.

"Maybe he's just wary of strangers," she said.

The accent indicated that English was her first language.

"Yes. Perhaps." I didn't add that his wariness was with good cause.

Kiki, uncharacteristically quiet, came around from behind her desk, took Miguel's hand, and led him to the back.

I looked at the woman. "I didn't catch your name."

"No, you didn't." She returned her attention to the magazine, flipping through the pages.

"Is there anything I can help you with?"

"I don't think so." She spoke without looking up.

• • •

I headed down the main hall, an extrawide walkway running through the middle of the building.

The Aztec Bazaar had its own unique smell, a heady mix of roasted corn, perfume, cooked onions, leather, and pine-scented cleaner.

The place was starting to smell comforting, like a home to me, and I wondered if Maria might be right. Maybe it was time to hit the road again. Then I thought about Miguel and his needs at the moment, one of which was to not be a drifter.

In the middle of the building was an open area used for meetings and get-togethers, blood drives, bake sales, and the occasional *lucha libre,* or Mexican wrestling matches.

Javier stood in the exact center of the area, looking up at the ceiling.

A man in his forties stood next to him, staring at the same spot. The man was vaguely Hispanic-looking, olive skin with reddish-brown hair.

Javier noticed my arrival. He called me over and introduced Frank Vega, the owner of the building that housed the Aztec Bazaar.

Vega squeezed my hand extra hard and told me in American-accented Spanish how nice it was to meet.

Before I could reply, he said, *"Perdona, hablas español?"*

"Está bien," I said. "I speak the language fairly well."

Vega wore faded jeans with holes in the knees, the fabric artfully torn so as to appear distressed but not worn out. On his feet was a pair of alligator-skin cowboy boots that probably cost a month's wages for the average customer of the bazaar. A black silk T-shirt covered by a tan linen sport coat completed the look of a *GQ* model sashaying into middle age.

He must have been connected to the expensively dressed woman in the office—and both had arrived in the Maserati currently occupying my parking space. Couldn't get much past a veteran investigator like me.

"A white guy who understands Spanish." He arched an eyebrow. "Isn't that something?"

Other than his clothes, Vega's most distinguishing characteristic was his height. Even with the heels on the boots, he was only five three or four, a good five inches shorter than Javier, who was three inches shorter than I.

Javier had previously told me about the landlord, a criminal defense attorney who had invested in real estate, buying properties in low-income parts of town. Vega was also an activist—Hispanic rights, immigrant issues—who'd been mentioned in the media of late as having a political future, perhaps running for a seat in the Texas Legislature or even the US House of Representatives.

Not bad, Javier used to say, for a half-Mexican boy from Waco.

I was curious if he'd get jeans without holes in them if he decided to run for office. Probably best not to ask.

"Mr. Vega and I were just talking about the roof," Javier said. "There's a leak. Whole thing needs to be replaced."

I looked up. The ceiling was discolored from what appeared to be water damage.

Vega said, "You know how to fix roofs, Señor Baines?"

I shook my head.

"That's a job for Mexicans, isn't it?" Vega's tone was on the edge of belligerent. He chuckled after a moment, presumably in an attempt to show he was just joking around.

"Or a roofer," I said. "Doesn't really matter if he's Mexican or not, does it?"

Vega stared at me, eyes like slits. I couldn't tell if there was something about me in particular he didn't like or if it was just gringos in general. On my end, ten seconds after meeting the man, I'd had enough of Frank Vega.

"Arlo handles security." Javier sounded nervous. "He's not involved in building maintenance."

"Security. Of course." Vega nodded. "What happened next door? Poor Mr. Sandoval."

"Last I heard, he was murdered," I said.

Vega looked at Javier. "He's a funny guy, your security man."

I wondered if it would be too impolite if I just walked away, then decided I didn't much care.

"Nice to meet you. I have work to do." I turned and headed toward the office.

Behind me, the sound of fingers snapping followed by Vega's voice: "Hold on. I'm not done talking to you yet."

I stopped, turned around as slowly as possible, and said, "And yet, I'm leaving anyway."

Vega's lips twisted into a frown. He flexed his fingers.

Javier stepped between us. He whispered, "*Por favor*, Arlo. A favor for me, OK?"

I took a deep breath, gave my best fake smile. "What can I do for you, Mr. Vega?"

"My wife. She needs to do some shopping. I'd appreciate it if you escorted her while she's on the premises." He paused. "Considering the crime around here."

Javier, still between us, looked at me, pleading with his eyes.

Vega crossed his arms. "You are a security guard, aren't you?"

A moment of silence.

"I'm not carrying her boxes," I said. "Just so we're clear on that."

- CHAPTER TEN -

The woman in the peach-colored dress was indeed Vega's wife, Quinn.

Quelle surprise, as they say in France.

We were in the office. The receptionist's desk was empty, Kiki and Miguel in the back somewhere.

Vega introduced me to her, Javier hovering behind him.

Quinn stood and shook my hand. "We saw each other earlier."

"Nice to put a name with a face," I said.

Vega cocked his head and stared at me.

"You wanted to look at the books." Javier touched his arm. "Let's go to my office and make ourselves comfortable."

Vega ignored him, spoke to me. "Take care of my wife, Mr. Baines."

Quinn rolled her eyes. "I'm fine."

"That's not what you said this morning."

She sighed heavily and picked up her purse, a small black handbag with a designer logo.

"There have been several robberies in our neighborhood," Vega said. "Home invasions. We're on edge, as to be expected."

"You'll be safe here," I said. "Very little crime at the Aztec Bazaar."

"Not counting Señor Sandoval," he said.

"Technically, that was next door."

"Technically." Vega continued to stare at my face without blinking, almost like he was challenging me to contradict him. "And you don't have any information on what happened or who is responsible?"

"No. I don't."

Vega and I locked eyeballs without speaking. His wife looked at the far wall, avoiding eye contact with anyone.

Finally, Javier said, "Arlo knows people at the police department. He's got his—how do you say?—ear to the dirt on this."

"Ground," I said. "The expression is 'ear to the ground.'"

Vega looked like he was about to reply, lips parted, finger raised in my direction, no doubt angry that a gringo was correcting his tenant.

Quinn cut him off. "It's OK, Frank. Let it go."

Vega glared at me for a moment longer and then lowered his finger, shoulders slumping forward slightly. In that moment, I realized that his aggression wasn't coming from a place of anger or a sense of superiority.

He was afraid.

I decided to take a shot in the dark. "Have you been threatened? Either of you?"

Silence. The barest hint of a glance between husband and wife.

"Of course not." Quinn stepped to the door. "My husband is just being overly cautious because of what's happened in our neighborhood. Are you ready, Mr. Baines?"

"Call me Arlo." I opened the door, motioned for her to go first. "After you."

• • •

50

Quinn Vega meandered down the main hall.

I followed a few steps behind, nodding hello to shopkeepers I knew.

At one of the western-wear stores, she browsed cowboy boots. I stood in the corner and exchanged looks with the clerk, a woman in her twenties, who appeared as confused as I was about why a person like Quinn Vega was perusing footwear at the Aztec Bazaar.

Quinn asked to try on several styles, spending a lot of time looking at herself in the mirror wearing a pair of chocolate, snip-toed boots that came to midcalf. Despite the odd juxtaposition—an expensive peach-colored sundress with brown boots—the ensemble worked. She looked good, cowboy chic. Not surprising when you thought about it. Quinn Vega had the lithe figure and demeanor of a fashion model. She'd probably look good in a burlap muumuu.

"What do you think?" She pivoted away from the mirror to face me, one leg—as elegant and shapely as her neck—extended.

I shrugged.

"Surely you have an opinion?"

"I'm not here to have an opinion. Just to keep an eye on you while you shop."

She chuckled like something was funny and turned to the clerk. "I'll take these."

The clerk ran her credit card while Quinn removed the boots. Three minutes later, we were back in the hallway, a shopping bag in her hand.

"What else is there to see at the Aztec Bazaar?" she asked.

"Plenty of things. You need some off-brand perfume? Or a statue of the Virgin Mary?"

"What I'd really like is a cup of coffee."

I led her around the corner to a kiosk that sold soft drinks and other beverages. She ordered coffee with cinnamon, and I got a bottle of water.

There was a bench across the hallway in front of a shop that sold discount wedding dresses. We sat at opposite ends, the shopping bag between us.

"You don't remember me, do you?" she said.

I paused with the bottle of water halfway to my lips.

That was a land mine of a question.

My life before getting married had been pretty typical of a male in his twenties—one long party, booze-soaked weekends, trying to sleep with anything that had a pulse. Was Frank Vega's wife part of that time?

I ran her face through my memory bank, came up empty. Her name was unique, but I only remembered one other Quinn, a girl from the class below me in high school. She'd been overweight, with thick glasses, stringy brown hair, and blotchy skin. Nothing about her had been elegant or shapely.

"I've changed a little since the last time we saw each other," she said.

I turned and looked at her, water bottle still poised in my hand.

"You remember now, don't you?" She took a sip of coffee. "Quinn Carmichael."

My mouth fell open.

"Algebra. We sat next to each other," she said. "I used to have the biggest crush on you."

I found my voice. "My gosh, how long has it been? Sorry, I didn't recognize you."

The eyes were familiar now. Hazel that looked brown in certain light. I recognized her jawline, too, angular and pointed. But everything else about her was different.

"Almost thirty years," she said. "You haven't changed much."

I trolled the recesses of my memory, dredging up what I could about Quinn Carmichael.

She'd been shy, blending in with the shadows. Despite a wealthy father, an Anglo, and a mother who'd been a Dallas Cowboys cheerleader, one of the first Latinas on the squad, Quinn had been teased unrelentingly by the popular girls because of her weight and looks.

Her junior year stuck in my mind, a family catastrophe of some sort. The father had lost his money, and the wife divorced him, as I recalled.

Another memory from that time period came to me. Quinn Carmichael, alone in the cafeteria, crying. Her father had just been indicted for some financial crime, embezzling or bank fraud. The popular girls had a lot of fun with that one.

"You were always nice to me," she said. "Back when others weren't."

I took a drink of water instead of responding, barely remembering ever talking to her, much less being nice.

"I heard about what happened to your family," she said. "I'm sorry for your loss."

"Thank you."

We were silent for a moment, both looking at each other but trying not to make eye contact.

"You were a police officer, last I heard. A Texas Ranger?"

I nodded.

She took a drink of coffee and watched the shoppers go by. The seconds stretched to a minute, and I wondered if that was what she really wanted to talk about instead of reminiscing about our high school days.

"Frank's line of work. He ends up associating with certain types of people who are, oh, let's just say not upstanding members of the community."

"They don't call it *criminal* defense for nothing," I said.

She stared at her container of coffee but didn't reply.

"Just the two of us," I said. "You can tell me whatever you want. Like if someone is making threats against you or your husband."

She put the coffee in the trash can next to her side of the bench as a woman pushing a stroller walked by, the baby crying its lungs out.

"It's not that easy," Quinn said. "Attorney-client, all that malarkey."

I waited.

"What do you know about the Sandoval murder?" she asked.

"Not a lot. Doesn't appear to be much physical evidence for the investigators to work with."

"Are you really in contact with the Dallas police department?" She turned and looked at me, her expression fearful. "Can you find out if they have a suspect?"

I thought about Fito's fingerprints and Throckmorton's interest.

"I have a source or two."

"I'm afraid whoever killed Sandoval might be after Frank."

"Why do you say that?"

She pursed her lips but didn't reply.

"If you want me to help, I need as much information as possible."

Silence.

"Whoever killed Sandoval," I said. "Do you think they're connected to the people threatening you?"

"I didn't say we were being threatened."

"You didn't have to."

She handed me a card. "If you find out any information about the killing, would you let me know? Please."

"It would help if you'd tell me what's going on."

She stood. "Frank's probably ready to go. Do you mind walking me back to the office?"

Ten minutes later, I watched Quinn and Frank Vega get into their expensive Italian sports car and leave.

I wondered how I could get in touch with Throckmorton. He seemed like the best source for information, and he obviously knew more than he let on yesterday.

I didn't really care that much about the crime next door, except in the abstract. I would help Quinn Carmichael Vega if I could, but what I really wanted was to learn as much as possible about Fito.

Protecting Miguel was my priority. Sandoval's murder, the threats against the Vegas, even security at the Aztec Bazaar, that was all secondary.

Turns out I didn't have to look very hard for Throckmorton.

He found me, right after the next murder.

- CHAPTER ELEVEN -

An hour later, after checking on Miguel, I was eating a fajita salad at the bar when Aloysius Throckmorton barged through the front door and beelined toward me, boots clacking on the concrete floor.

It was Friday, a little after noon, so the place was doing a pretty steady business, people hanging out, drinking beer, watching soccer on one of the TVs.

Throckmorton, eyes bloodshot like he hadn't slept much the night before, pointed an index finger at my face.

"You and me," he said. *"Vámonos."*

"What's up?" I stabbed a piece of lettuce with my fork. "You got anything on Fito?"

"Outside. Now."

I pointed to my food. "How about after I finish?"

He leaned close. "How many of your amigos in here are legal, do you think?"

I didn't answer. Not very many, if I had to guess.

"You want me to call immigration and we'll find out?"

"Who pissed in your Rice Krispies?" I pushed my plate away.

He looked around the room, lowered his voice. "There's been another murder, just like the one yesterday."

• • •

La Cocina de Mariscos was a seafood restaurant five blocks south of the Aztec Bazaar.

The place was part drive-in, part sit-down, a covered parking area with slots for a dozen or so cars, tables for about that many inside.

I'd eaten there several times. They served a mean fried shrimp platter.

Throckmorton and I were in his Suburban across the street, idling in the parking lot of a dollar store.

Crime scene tape circled the entire property where the restaurant was located. Forensic investigators scurried about, along with a number of uniformed officers and a couple of people in plain clothes, one of whom was Ross.

"An hour ago," Throckmorton said. "The owner takes the trash out. He doesn't come back, so a waitress goes looking for him. Finds him in the alley, three rounds in the head."

"Let me guess. A small-caliber weapon, and nobody heard anything."

He nodded.

Two murders in twenty-four hours, only a few blocks apart. Not unusual in this zip code, but the similar MO wasn't giving me the warm fuzzies.

We were both silent for a few moments.

He drummed his fingers on the steering wheel. "I'm sorry for the way everything played out back when."

He was referring to the deaths of the people who'd killed my family and the subsequent investigation, how he'd come after me like a hooker for a sailor on shore leave. Relentless, as unstoppable as the tides, until someone else confessed to the crime.

I thought about all the different ways to reply, various retorts that sprang to mind. I decided to keep it simple.

"Thanks for saying so."

A small photograph like an old-style wallet photo from high school was stuck to the clear plastic under the dash, just between the speedometer and the tach.

He pulled the photo off the plastic, rubbed it against his shirt like he was removing dust. Then he placed the picture back where it had been. The image was that of a young woman.

"Who's in the picture?" I asked.

He ignored my question. "The DPS needs an asset. Somebody off the books."

"Why are you talking like a spook?"

"These aren't the only two murders, Arlo."

I didn't say anything.

"At least two before this in Dallas," he said. "Maybe more. Plus one in Hillsboro."

Hillsboro was a town about an hour south of the city, straddling Interstate 35, a NAFTA superhighway that ran from Laredo up to the Canadian border, the backbone of the country.

"I read your file yesterday," he said. "You were a damn good investigator."

"You get that I already have a job, right?"

"Sandoval and the guy across the street, they're not something that the Texas Rangers would normally be involved with."

I waited, wondering where he was going with this, telling me something I already knew.

The Rangers handled plenty of murder cases, but most were in unincorporated areas of the state or small municipalities without a dedicated homicide department. There would be little reason for the organization to be involved in a crime like this in a city such as Dallas.

He continued. "But Austin wants eyes on these investigations."

"You think there's a reason the police can't handle the job?"

"I think the more people looking at this, the better. That's why I want to hire you." He mentioned a daily pay rate. "DPS has some discretionary funds available. You'd be paid in cash, of course."

Neither of us spoke for a few seconds. The coroner's van pulled up across the street.

"What's so special about these murders?" I asked.

"The two victims you know about, Sandoval and the restaurant guy. Put on your investigator hat; describe them to me."

I thought about it for a moment and then told him what I knew about Alejandro Sandoval and the man who owned the seafood joint. Both were small-time businessmen, immigrants from Mexico, hardworking people. Responsible. Industrious.

"How much do you think Sandoval pulled down at the tire store?" he asked.

"Small place like that, maybe he grosses a couple of hundred K a year." I shrugged. "He's probably taking home fifty or sixty thousand."

Throckmorton opened the console of his truck and retrieved a file marked with the logo of the Drug Enforcement Administration. He fished out an eight-by-ten picture and handed it to me, an image obviously taken with a telephoto lens.

The photograph, also marked with a DEA stamp, showed a house on a hill, an enormous place that looked like a Miami Beach brothel, white stucco and palm trees, a multicolored tile roof. A circular driveway curved in front of the structure, dominated by a fountain containing statues of three apparently life-size horses running through the water.

"Sandoval's legal residence is a shack in Pleasant Grove," Throckmorton said. "You know that part of town, don't you? The butthole of Dallas."

I pointed to the photo. "Then what's this?"

"That's his weekend crib, up in Denton County. Horse country. Wife paid one-point-nine mil for it."

I looked across the street again. The restaurant was small and wood framed, peeling white paint on the walls, a pitched roof that looked like it needed to be redone. A modest place, almost a dump, not unlike the tire store.

"Sandoval and the guy across the street." Throckmorton paused. "The intel I'm getting, looks like they're affiliated with the Vaqueros."

I swore, felt my heartbeat ratchet up a notch.

The Vaqueros were the dominant narco traffickers along the Rio Grande, ultraviolent, even by the standards of drug cartels.

The organization had been founded by an ex-priest turned rancher who ran the group like a paramilitary religious order, their activities part of a higher calling.

A favorite trick of the Vaqueros was the forced conversion of their enemies by full immersion baptism. Not all that bad, except for the fact they used acid instead of water.

"Are you sure?" I said. "Sandoval's been here for years. He's probably owned that tire store longer than the Vaqueros have been in existence."

He tossed the photo of the garish house on the console and gave me a deadpan stare.

The cartel had started in Reynosa less than a decade ago, a small town across from McAllen, near the Gulf of Mexico.

From there the Vaqueros had spread like a pandemic along the river, making inroads as far west as the Juarez / El Paso area. But as far as I knew, neither they nor any other cartel had a significant presence beyond the border region. The distribution side of the business was left to local groups.

"The DEA is convinced this is shaping up to be a turf war," he said. "Two groups making a play for Dallas."

I looked up and down the street, seeing everything with fresh eyes, shopkeepers and customers, parents and children, people living their lives, minding their own business.

What Throckmorton described was law enforcement's worst-case scenario, the violence that had plagued the border for years advancing northward. If that actually occurred, nothing would be the same in this city.

"Everybody wants to run silent on this," he said. "You can understand why."

I certainly could. This wasn't exactly chamber of commerce material: *Come for the mild winters. Stay for the narco-trafficker wars.* Widespread panic would erupt if word got out that two cartels were about to go *Scarface* on the streets of the city.

"You still haven't told me why you need someone else working on this," I said.

Throckmorton scratched his mustache with an index finger, refusing to look in my direction, hand shaking slightly.

"No-no-no." I shook my head. "Please don't say there's a leak."

"Potentially." He paused. "Maybe."

"Tell me what happened."

"We had intel. One of the *jefes* was coming across the river. Guy called his cousin in Dallas, said he'd be in town in a couple of days."

Not many people were aware of the fact, but the Texas Rangers ran a surprisingly sophisticated intelligence operation along the Rio Grande.

The Border Security Operations Center, nicknamed B-Sock, disseminated a large amount of information to law enforcement agencies across the state as well as to a number of federal organizations.

"We even had eyes on him," Throckmorton said. "He was traveling with an entourage, easy to track, so B-Sock sends a memo to the DEA, who in turn tells the Dallas police. Two hours later, the crew scattered like a busted covey of quail, everybody hightailing it back to Mexico."

We stared at the restaurant for a moment.

"How many people know you and I are talking?" I asked.

"Only me. Nothing written down, either." He shifted in his seat and looked me in the eyes. "Can I count on you?"

A moment passed, neither of us speaking.

"Aren't you getting tired of babysitting that drunk Mexican?" he asked.

"Javier's my friend."

"So you don't miss being a cop?"

I looked out the side window at the traffic speeding down the street but didn't say anything. Part of me did miss working as a Texas Ranger, and he could no doubt sense it. The thrill of the hunt, spending your time on things that really mattered. Belonging to something bigger than yourself.

Across the street, the four-door Maserati that had been parked in my spot earlier screeched to a stop by the curb, right behind one of the squad cars.

Throckmorton grabbed a pair of binoculars from under the seat. "What have we here?"

A very short man in a tan sport coat exited the driver's side of the Maserati.

"That's Frank Vega." I explained who he was and how Vega's wife wanted to get the inside scoop on Sandoval's murder, afraid her husband was in danger.

Vega must have heard about the latest killing and decided to find out what he could on his own.

"A criminal defense attorney." Throckmorton spat out the words, using the same tone as if he were talking about a nun rapist.

Like most cops, he despised lawyers, especially those who worked for people accused of committing crimes.

Vega approached the yellow tape. One of the other plainclothes officers motioned for him to stay back. A conversation ensued, Vega waving his arms about, the cop shrugging every now and then. Vega continued to harangue the officer, finally touching him on the shoulder.

Throckmorton chuckled. "That was a mistake."

An instant later, Frank Vega lay facedown on the ground, hands cuffed behind his back. A few seconds after that, the Maserati's passenger door opened, and Quinn Vega got out.

"Yowza." Throckmorton kept the binoculars pressed to his eyes. "That's a spicy enchilada."

"Why don't you tell Ross to cut Vega loose?"

He lowered the binoculars. "Now why would I want to do that?"

Because Frank Vega getting arrested would only muddy the waters. Because even though he was an arrogant prick, going to jail wouldn't make him less so. Because Quinn Vega seemed like she'd been through the wringer of late, and I didn't think this would help her emotional state.

I didn't say any of that. Instead, I opened the door and started to exit the vehicle. "Fine, I'll take care of it."

"Ah, I get it." He smiled. "Damsel in distress, Arlo Baines saves the day."

I stopped with one foot on the pavement, a wave of anger washing over me, the son of a bitch more right than I wanted to admit.

"Before you skedaddle, let's talk about the fingerprints on the beer can," Throckmorton said. "Or did you forget about those?"

I hadn't forgotten. That topic was number one on my to-do list . . . just as soon as I extricated Frank Vega from his current situation.

"Guy's name is Alphonso Alvarez," Throckmorton said. "Goes by Fito."

"And?"

"And he's a cop."

- CHAPTER TWELVE -

I gripped the side of the Suburban's door, stared at Throckmorton.

"A cop?"

"Del Rio PD." He paused. "Currently taking a leave of absence."

Across the street, Quinn Vega was yelling at the plainclothes officer while her husband lay facedown on the pavement.

"What does that mean?" I asked. "Leave of absence?"

"I don't know. And that's not making me a happy camper."

Ross, hands on his hips, was now speaking with Quinn. The other plainclothes officer pulled Frank Vega from the ground.

"I thought you were gonna help that human skid mark," Throckmorton said.

"In a minute. Tell me what else you know about Fito."

"That's all I got. Whatever happened down there, it's buried deep."

He looked like he had more to say. Instead he stared at the seafood restaurant and drummed his fingers on the steering wheel.

"You're holding back," I said. "What else do you have?"

"I used a terminal at the DEA office to run a check on the guy. Now my username and password won't work."

The other plainclothes officer led Vega to a squad car, Quinn watching helplessly.

"Don't leave without me." I shut the door and headed to the crime scene, threading my way through the traffic.

• • •

Quinn Vega had her back to the street, talking to Ross.

Ross looked at me over her shoulder and said, "You again?"

"Is that really necessary?" I pointed to the squad car with Vega in the back.

"Second one of my crime scenes in two days you've shown up at," Ross said. "That's getting kinda weird, don't you think?"

"Arlo, please." Quinn touched my arm. "Can you help? They've arrested Frank."

I spoke to Ross. "Cut him loose. Vega's just upset. He didn't mean any harm."

"Upset, was he?" Ross arched an eyebrow. "You want to know how many cases I've watched circle the toilet because of Frank Vega?"

The other plainclothes officer came up behind his partner. He crossed his arms, stared at me.

"OK, we'll play it your way," I said. "Vega assaulted your guy. I was a witness. Let's call the DA right now and get charges filed."

Quinn's face drained of color. Ross and the other officer didn't say anything. Their eyes narrowed.

Transporting Frank Vega to the county jail, filling out the paperwork, getting an assistant district attorney assigned to the case—all of that would take hours, time both investigators would rather spend working on the new murder.

A few moments passed. The other detective whispered in Ross's ear. Ross whispered back. Then he looked at me. "You're a piece of work, Baines. Whose side are you on, anyway?"

"What's happening?" Quinn asked. "I don't understand."

"Wait in your car," I said.

She looked at me and then at the two homicide detectives. After a moment, she walked back to the Maserati and got in the driver's side.

The other officer muttered under his breath but headed toward the rear of the squad car.

"Happy now?" Ross asked.

"Tell me about the new murder. Is there video?"

"You really think I'm giving you anything?"

"We're on the same team," I said. "We both want to find whoever killed these men."

"Go back and play cowboys and Indians with your Texas Ranger buddy. I'm gonna count to ten, and if you're still here, I'll trade you out for Vega."

I wondered if Ross could be the leak. He'd been a cop for nearly three decades, exposed to every kind of corruption imaginable. Had someone gotten to him?

"Was it the same caliber as Sandoval?" I asked. "Just tell me that."

"I'm not kidding, Baines. Get the hell out of here."

• • •

Inside the Suburban, Throckmorton turned the AC to high while I wiped sweat off my face. Across the street, Vega's Maserati pulled away from the curb and sped off as Ross stood watching us.

"He's giving me the freeze-out." I related what happened.

Throckmorton pointed to the glove compartment. "In there. Something for you."

I twisted the latch, looked inside.

On top of the instruction manuals for the SUV lay a folded sheet of paper.

I opened the paper and saw a picture of a picture, an image on a screen that appeared to have been taken with a cell phone.

This wasn't anything official, like the photo of Sandoval's place.

The picture captured a list of names, fuzzy and indistinct, Hispanic-sounding, all men, handwritten on a sheet of lined notepaper. There were seven of them, the third from the top Alejandro Sandoval. The fourth was the owner of the restaurant.

"Those mean anything to you?" He put the SUV in gear, pulled on to the street.

"The two dead ones, Alejandro Sandoval and the restaurant guy, do. Who are the rest?"

He didn't reply, stopping at a light.

A *paletero* man pushing an insulated cart filled with Popsicles and ice cream bars trudged across the intersection. A homeless guy shuffled along behind him, holding his pants up with one hand, the other pointing skyward like he was Moses leading the Israelites across the Red Sea.

"Where'd you get this?" I asked.

"The DEA, the working-together thing, spirit of cooperation—that's not going so well."

I realized he was talking about more than just his log-in info not working.

"It rarely does."

"I'm getting the deep freeze, too," he said. "Probably didn't help when I started nosing around after your boy Fito."

"Sorry," I said, not sorry at all.

"Nearest I can tell, the feds had somebody undercover with either the Vaqueros or one of their competitors. Whoever the guy was, he sent that picture to his handler. I managed to get a shot during one of the last briefings they let me sit in on."

I looked at the list again. The name after the owner of the restaurant was Juan Gonzalez, the Mexican equivalent of John Smith.

Horns honked behind us. The intersection was clear.

"The guy above Sandoval, he's the victim in Hillsboro." Throckmorton pressed the gas. "The one above him has the same name as a mechanic in South Dallas who was shot two weeks ago."

"It's a hit list."

"Apparently. Either people who work for the Vaqueros or are in their way somehow. Maybe they're with another organization."

"What happened to the undercover guy? He still a viable source?"

A pronounced silence.

"I got two months to go," he said. "Then I'm pulling the plug on the DPS."

"Good for you. Now tell me about the undercover guy."

"I want to stop this narco bullshit. Keep it down south where it belongs." He paused. "Whatever it takes."

I waited. He wouldn't be the first law enforcement officer willing to bend/break/mutilate the rules for the greater good.

A DPD squad car, lights flashing, sped down the street toward the seafood restaurant.

"Little village south of Nuevo Laredo," he said. "A few days after that picture arrived, the army found the undercover guy nailed to a cross in the town square."

Neither of us spoke for a couple of blocks.

"They figured it took him half a day to die." He pulled into the Aztec Bazaar's parking lot and stopped by the front entrance. "I'll be in touch."

●　·●　●

I found Javier sitting at the bar, a half-empty bottle of Modelo in front of him.

"Where has my gringo friend been today?" He took a long drink.

"There's been another murder."

"La Cocina de Mariscos." He twirled the bottle above his head. "The talk of the bar."

"How well did you know Sandoval?" I asked.

He didn't reply. His eyes narrowed.

"Is it possible that he was a narco?"

"No. He was a good man."

"Are you sure?"

He took another drink. "These days, I am not sure about anything. No one but God knows what lurks in a man's soul."

I took the bottle from his hand, placed it out of reach. "No more preaching about the human condition. Sandoval and the guy who owned the restaurant. Could they be part of a cartel?"

He cocked his head. "Why are you asking me this, Arlo?"

I told him about Throckmorton and the DEA, how there'd been a series of murders, seemingly innocent people except that they appeared to be affiliated with the Vaqueros. Or maybe a competing organization. Or just innocents caught up in events they never saw coming.

"You're going to work for the police again?" His tone was thick with disdain.

"Somebody's out there killing Mexicans. People like you. I'd want to find out who."

"People like me?" Anger flashed in his eyes. "You think I'm a narco?"

"You know what I mean."

He didn't respond for a few moments. Then he said, "This Throckmorton person. He's the man who was in here last night, the Texas Ranger?"

I nodded.

"Why do you want to be part of that again?"

I didn't answer. He wouldn't grasp something I had trouble putting into words myself.

"While you have been with your *policía* friend, have you learned anything about Fito?"

This was a tricky juncture, Fito's real identity. There was little sense in getting Javier more stirred up, so I decided to lie to my friend for the first time.

"Not yet."

A moment of silence. Javier stared at me, his expression blank.

"Where's Miguel?" I asked.

"The office. Torres showed up a little while ago. They're going to see a movie later." He motioned to the bartender for another beer.

Thank God for small favors and tough old marines like Javier's neighbor.

I said, "Don't drink any more today, OK?"

The bartender, eyebrows raised, held a fresh beer in his hand and looked at his boss. Javier was drinking more than usual, and his level of moroseness seemed to be higher than normal.

"Why do you care?"

"Oh, I don't know." I shrugged. "Miguel shouldn't see you drunk. It's bad for business. I don't want to watch you commit slow suicide . . . Pick a reason."

He waved off the bartender, who put the bottle down behind the bar.

"What the hell is wrong with you?" I asked.

"I told you yesterday." He pushed the beer away. "Evil is headed our way."

- CHAPTER THIRTEEN -

I sat in my pickup and entered Alejandro Sandoval's home address into my phone's GPS.

Miguel and Torres stood by the main entrance to the Aztec Bazaar, customers coming and going around them.

I waved at Miguel.

He waved back and gave me a weak smile. Then he and Torres went inside.

I cranked the ignition and pulled out of my parking spot. Twenty minutes later, in the far southeastern part of the city, I turned off Lake June Road and onto a narrow residential street.

Pleasant Grove was not far from the Great Trinity Forest, a large wooded floodplain noted for its abundance of wildlife and places to hide bodies. Maybe that's where the "grove" part had come from, all the trees. I was drawing a blank on the "pleasant" part, however.

The neighborhood was one of the poorest in the city, making the area around the Aztec Bazaar look like Rodeo Drive in comparison.

Little in the way of jobs or other economic opportunities, lots of gang activities and street crime.

Alejandro Sandoval's house sat behind a small strip center that contained a place that made payday loans and a furniture rental store.

The one-story home—a FOR SALE sign by the curb—was small but well kept, brick painted a pale gray, the lawn freshly mowed, a few flowers in the beds. Vehicles filled the driveway that ran along the side of the house, the last one a navy-blue Suburban with Mexican license plates.

I parked near the end of the block by a house with plywood over the windows. Two elementary-school-age girls played in the dirt that passed for the front yard.

Directly across from where I parked was an elderly Toyota Camry, the front windows rolled down. The car was in such a place that it offered a clear view of the Sandoval house.

A Hispanic man in his twenties sat behind the wheel, smoking a cigarette, his neck and face streaked with tattoos. He was skinny, bony shoulders prominent because of the wifebeater T-shirt he wore.

He watched me get out of my truck, never breaking eye contact, a sneer on his lips.

Gangbanger 101—show how tough you are without lifting a finger.

I ignored him and headed toward Alejandro Sandoval's home.

On the front stoop, I could hear the sounds of people inside, the murmur of conversation, the *clink* of plates.

The door opened before I could knock, and one of Sandoval's sons appeared in the entryway. The younger one, about fifteen as I recalled. His eyes were red like he'd been crying.

"*Mis sentidas condolencias,*" I said. *My deepest condolences.*

He stared at me blankly.

"Is your mother here?" I asked. "*Está tu madre aquí?*"

A woman appeared behind him.

Delores Sandoval, Alejandro's widow.

I remembered her as an attractive woman in her early forties, dark hair shiny like in a shampoo commercial. Now she looked old before her time. Her face was puffy, deep lines around her eyes, skin an unhealthy pallor, hair dull and lifeless, streaked with gray.

She told her son to go inside, then looked at me, waiting.

"Señora Sandoval," I said. *"Yo trabajo en el Aztec Bazaar."*

"I know who you are." She spoke without an accent, her English flawless, unlike her late husband.

"Please accept my sympathy for your loss."

She worked as a schoolteacher, first or second grade, as I recalled. She possessed a certain amount of refinement, something that had stood in contrast to her blue-collar husband.

The attraction of opposites, one of life's great mysteries.

"Thank you." She nodded once.

"Forgive this intrusion, but would you be able to talk to me for a few minutes about your husband's death?"

Her lips pressed together, a frown creasing her face.

"That's always been a safe neighborhood," I said. "The police, well, you know how they are. Sometimes regular people have to do what they can to make sure no one else gets hurt."

She stared at me for a moment and then stepped aside, holding the door open.

The entrance went straight into a small living/dining area. Shag carpet, wood-paneled walls, overstuffed sofas facing a television.

Every seat was filled with people, mostly women. Some were talking softly; some were eating. They all stopped what they were doing and stared at me. Sadness filled the room like smoke in a tavern.

Delores Sandoval pointed toward the rear of the house. "Let's go to the back."

I followed her into a kitchen outfitted by Montgomery Ward some-time in the seventies. Formica countertops the color of avocados, a harvest-gold refrigerator, worn linoleum flooring.

The room smelled like food and coffee. Platters covered a small table in a breakfast nook—tamales, a ham, pasta salads, brownies, chips and salsa.

The son who had answered the door was there with several men, two of whom I recognized from the tire store. They all looked at me but didn't speak.

A door leading to the rear yard was next to a washer and dryer on the far wall.

I pointed to the door. "Perhaps we could go outside? Find some-where private to talk."

Delores shook her head. "It's best if we stay here."

The son said, "Mama, are you all right?"

She nodded. "Go check on everyone in the living room."

The son glared at me but did as he was told, the other men trailing after him. When they were gone, Delores motioned for us to sit at the table covered with food.

"Do you know about my family?" I asked.

She frowned, shook her head.

I told her about my wife and two children, how they were mur-dered one afternoon at the home we shared. How I felt at the time, the numbness giving way to grief, a pain I still carried with me to this day.

"I thought you wanted to talk about the neighborhood," she said, "not grief."

I decided to be direct. "I'm sorry to do this now, but I need you to tell me about the house in Denton County."

She rolled her eyes, a look on her face somewhere between amuse-ment and disgust.

"What a question," she said. "You Americans talk about how you like people getting ahead, but when a Mexican does just that, there must be something illegal going on."

"I never mentioned anything illegal."

"There was no need," she said. "I understood what you were implying."

"Where did the money come from for the house in Denton County?"

"Alejandro Sandoval was a good man. A good husband." She paused. "My father gave us the money. He has a construction company in El Paso."

She seemed exasperated. Her tone had become shrill.

I made a mental note to have Throckmorton do a deep dive on her family.

"I suppose you think every Italian is in the mafia?" she said.

"Not at all." I paused. "But there's a saying about smoke and fire. Perhaps you're familiar with it."

A moment passed.

"The next block over is gang territory," she said. "They sell drugs openly. My children have to walk to school and see that every day."

I waited.

"We wanted to get away from that."

The sign in the yard. I wondered if they were moving to the Denton County house or somewhere else.

"Do you think the gangbangers on the next block killed your husband?" I asked.

She pinched the bridge of her nose, chest heaving, the effort of holding it together obvious. Tears welled in her eyes, and she began to cry.

I stood and walked to the sink, feeling like a big, steaming pile of shit for questioning her right now. As I filled a glass with water, I glanced out the window overlooking the backyard.

Two Hispanic men in their thirties stood on a small patio at the rear of the yard. The men wore polo shirts and expensive-looking jeans. They were on either side of Alejandro's older son, Ernesto, a senior in high school, the man of the house now.

The two individuals carried themselves differently from the group of mourners assembled in the living room. They weren't grieving. They were there for business.

One of the men had a birthmark on his cheek, a dark splotch about the size of a matchbook. He handed Ernesto a beer. Another patted him on the shoulder.

I took the water to Delores and sat back down, grateful for the heft of the Glock in my waistband.

She accepted the glass and took a long drink.

"Who are the men in your backyard?" I asked.

She put the glass down, crossed her arms again. "I'm not part of any of that."

"Any of what?"

No reply.

"Are they business associates of your husband's?"

She didn't say anything. After a moment she nodded, a glum look on her face.

"Tell me about them," I said.

"He wanted the best for his family. You can understand that, can't you?"

I nodded.

"Those men. They needed someone to handle their, uh, tire business."

"Of course," I said. "They look like the kind of people who take a lot of pride in their vehicles."

We were both silent for a few moments. No noise in the kitchen except for the refrigerator humming.

"I know what Alejandro was involved in was wrong." She looked toward the back door. "But there was so much money. How could he turn that down?"

Because money wasn't free. The more that was on the table, the higher the risk. Ask any hedge fund manager. Or cartel boss.

"Do you think those men outside had anything to do with your husband's murder?"

She shook her head, then pursed her lips like she was choosing her words with great deliberation. "They were always nice," she said. "Pleasant and respectful."

I was sure they were. Pablo Escobar was supposed to be a great guy to pal around with, too, at least until you crossed him.

"Did Alejandro ever have any disagreements with those men?"

"No. Never."

I believed her. Somehow I didn't see Sandoval doing anything to mess up the money machine. Certainly nothing like skimming or otherwise screwing over his bosses. He was a straight arrow, at least by the standards of people who get in bed with drug smugglers.

"They told me it was a mugging," she said. "Just a random crime."

Of course they did. Because they wanted to keep a lid on this as much as anybody.

She took another drink of water, holding the glass in two hands like it might drop.

"Do you know about the other murders?" I asked.

She frowned.

"Several people have been killed under circumstances similar to your husband." I paused. "People who were perhaps affiliated with the same organization."

Her eyes grew wide.

"Your sons," I said. "Are they involved, too?"

Her face turned pale, breath coming in deep heaves.

I put one of my cards on the table by a bowl of queso. "That has my cell number. If you want to talk, give me a call."

"Are my children in danger?"

"What do you think?"

She covered her mouth with one hand and looked toward the back door.

- CHAPTER FOURTEEN -

I left Delores Sandoval in the kitchen. Nodded goodbye to her youngest son in the living room, exited the front door.

The Toyota from the end of the street was parked in the driveway now, blocking the sidewalk. The gangbanger stood by the front, arms crossed.

He had a friend with him, Fito, which didn't surprise me at all.

"Howdy," I said. "What's up, *muchachos*?"

Fito pointed to the Toyota. "Let's take a ride."

"I don't think so."

"Don't make this hard." He massaged his thumb. "You don't want to piss me off any more than you already have."

"Then why don't you go back to Del Rio, and we can avoid the whole issue."

He furrowed his brow like he was processing the fact that I knew where he was from.

"You work for the Vaqueros?" I asked. "Or someone else?"

The gangbanger took a deep breath, eyes wide. Fito sighed like a parent does with a toddler who won't pick up his toys.

"You and me," he said. "Ever consider we might be on the same page?"

"Not for a moment."

"I'm an investigator." He paused. "Like you used to be."

"So who are you working for, Mr. Investigator?"

"That's not how this goes, you asking me questions."

My truck was five houses away. A twenty-second walk, if no one was chasing me.

"These were honest, hardworking people who were murdered," he said. "My employers just want to find out who's responsible."

I didn't say anything.

"I was close yesterday," he said. "Damn shame. Alejandro, he was a good man."

I thought about the three people in the Sandoval backyard. "Do your employers wear polo shirts and fancy jeans?"

"Those guys? Strictly middle management. My boss is not based in this area. Yet."

Behind me came the screech of a door opening, followed by the sound of voices. The voices trailed off, and two women appeared in my peripheral vision, walking at an angle across the front yard, trying to avoid our little confab.

"The thing is," Fito said, "we got too many cooks in the kitchen. You coming here, muddying the waters, asking questions."

The women strode down the sidewalk, glancing over their shoulders as they went.

"Here's what's gonna happen," he said. "You and me are going somewhere private. You're gonna tell me why you're so interested in what's going on and what you've found out so far."

I reached under my T-shirt and pulled the Glock from my waistband, aiming the muzzle at his face.

"I'm leaving," I said. "That's what's gonna happen."

"You think one gun's gonna get you out of this mess?"

Down the block, the two women got into an old Chevy Blazer.

Whoop-whoop-whoop-whoop.

The vehicle's alarm triggered, distracting my attention for a nanosecond, which was long enough for Fito to produce a gun and point it at me.

"You almost broke my thumb yesterday," he said. "Don't give me another reason to shoot you. Get in the car."

The gangbanger pulled out a pistol as well, and now it was two against one.

I weighed my options, tried to divine if either one of them would actually fire at me on a residential street in the middle of the afternoon.

"Think about Miguel," Fito said. "Do the right thing for the boy. Get in the car."

I tightened my grip on the Glock. My vision turned red at the edges, stomach churning.

Fito grinned. "Ooh. Struck a nerve."

"I told you to leave the boy out of this."

"You even know his last name?" he asked.

"Ortega. Miguel Ortega."

"And you know about his parents?"

I didn't answer, just kept the gun aimed at his face.

"Did you know that after they died, he ended up with a gang who did work for the organization based in Sinaloa?"

The missing weeks before we'd found him in the Dallas bus station. He'd been with another cartel.

"Maybe you figured that out," he said. "But I bet you didn't know that they used him as a shooter."

The muzzle of my gun wavered as the air around me turned cold. The street looked different all of a sudden, alien, the colors and shapes wrong.

"People don't pay attention to kids." Fito chuckled. "In and out, bang-bang, you're dead."

Maria was right. The bad always corrupted the good. Water seeking a path down. It was the nature of things.

"He ever spends the night with you, I'd sleep with one eye open," Fito said. "That boy's a killer. Now drop your weapon and get in the car before I shoot you in the knee."

A black Suburban appeared, coming from the end of the block where the women had accidentally set off their car alarm. I hadn't noticed, what with the two thugs aiming guns at me and my mind trying to process what I'd just learned about Miguel.

Throckmorton's rig.

The Suburban stopped in the middle of the street, right behind the Toyota.

Fito and the gangbanger lowered their guns slightly, their attention split between the big SUV and me.

Throckmorton got out and ambled around the front of his vehicle, hand resting on the butt of his pistol, badge gleaming in the sun.

He said, "Put the guns down, amigos."

The gangbanger looked at Fito. A moment later he knelt and placed his pistol on the pavement, standing up with his hands raised.

Fito turned his head and spoke to the Texas Ranger. "This doesn't concern you."

"Lower your weapon." Throckmorton popped the safety restraint on his holster. "I'm not fooling around here, *comprende?*"

"I'm a police officer," Fito said.

"Good for you, señor." Throckmorton unholstered his pistol, a stainless-steel Colt 1911. "Now do like I told you."

Fito glared at me. He licked his lips and lowered the gun to his side.

I stuck my Glock back in my waistband and picked up the gangbanger's piece. I reached for Fito's gun with my free hand but stopped when Throckmorton said, "Not him."

Fito smiled.

"What the hell are you talking about?" My hand was poised a few inches from Fito's weapon.

"Get in the truck, Arlo." Throckmorton nodded toward his Suburban.

"Yes, Arlo." Fito continued to smile. "Get in the truck."

I gripped the gangbanger's weapon so hard my knuckles hurt. It would be so easy. Raise the gun, squeeze the trigger, one round right through Fito's eye.

He must have sensed my thoughts because he stopped smiling and took a step back.

Throckmorton said, "Quit jacking around, Arlo. Just walk away."

My vision blurred. I remembered the last Christmas with my wife and children—the tree, the presents, the brisket on the smoker in the backyard.

The gun felt hot in my hand.

I raised the weapon.

"Arlo." Throckmorton moved a step closer. "Put the gun down and get in the damn truck, *now.*"

Fito's eyes widened as his face paled.

I lowered the weapon, never breaking eye contact with Fito. After a moment, I strode to the Suburban and jumped in the passenger seat.

Cold air blasted from the AC vents. I shivered, my clothes soaked with sweat.

An instant later, Throckmorton hopped behind the wheel, yanked the transmission into drive. I could see Fito and the gangbanger on the sidewalk watching us.

Throckmorton jammed on the gas. "What the hell's wrong with you?"

"Why didn't you arrest them?"

He swore, sped past my pickup, tires screeching as he made the turn onto the cross street.

"Miguel," I said. "Did you know?"

"What are you talking about?"

I stared out the window without seeing anything, the gangbanger's gun still in my hand.

"We need to talk," Throckmorton said. "This is getting sticky."

"What do you mean?"

"Your boy Fito. He's working for the DEA."

- CHAPTER FIFTEEN -

Throckmorton pulled in to the parking lot of a liquor store a few blocks away, slapped the transmission into park.

"What do you mean he works for the DEA?" I asked.

"Fito Alvarez is something called a 'specialized intelligence resource,'" he said.

The term sounded like a fancy name for a paid informant.

"What the hell does that mean?"

Throckmorton arched an eyebrow. "What do you think it means?"

I related what Fito had just told me, how he was investigating the murders as well, apparently for the Vaqueros, which meant the killings were the result of a turf war like Throckmorton had thought.

"So he's playing both sides," Throckmorton said. "Wonder whose team he's really on?"

I took his question to be rhetorical. It didn't take a degree in psychology to grasp that Fito's ultimate loyalty lay with the cartel, the highest bidder, an organization that lost more money in a week to termites and silverfish than the average police officer earned in a year.

We were both silent for a few moments. My limbs felt heavy as the adrenaline bled from my system.

"Came awful close to punching that guy's ticket back there," Throckmorton said. "You better double up on your blood pressure medicine."

I could still see Fito's look of surprise as he realized how close I was to shooting him. So much for choosing not to be angry.

"Do you know anything else about him?" I asked. "Like why he's not in uniform down in Del Rio?"

Throckmorton shook his head. "And I've asked. One too many times."

A guy in a blue work shirt with a Jiffy Lube logo on the breast emerged from the liquor store carrying a brown paper sack. He eyed the Suburban and then got into an old Camaro.

"A suit from the Justice Department came to the office," Throckmorton said. "Got all up in my business, wanting to know why I'm so interested in Detective Alvarez. I told him the guy was trying to date my niece, which I think he believed for about a millisecond."

It was easy to understand why the feds were touchy about Fito. They obviously knew he was working for the cartel in addition to being on Uncle Sam's payroll. They no doubt rationalized the arrangement in their usual fashion—he would lead to a bigger fish.

The problem with the "bigger fish" theory was that it so seldom panned out. Also, there was the issue of what would happen if knowledge of their arrangement ever became public. Fito's résumé would not play well at a senate subcommittee hearing.

"Next thing I know, Austin calls and tells me I'm off the task force."

I digested that bit of information for a moment and then told him about the conversation with Sandoval's widow. I also told him about the two men in the backyard with the older son and the SUV with Mexican plates.

"That's not good," he said. "Management's in town."

I didn't say anything. My thoughts were a jumble, my brain trying to come to terms with the kind of people who would use a child as a hit man.

"Who's Miguel?" Throckmorton pulled the picture of the young woman off the plastic by the speedometer, dusted it again.

"What?"

"Earlier. You said, 'Miguel. Did you know?'"

"Never mind. It's not important."

He returned the picture to its place and gave me a quizzical look. Then he pulled back on to the street.

"How'd you know where I'd be?" I asked.

"After I got reamed out by the DOJ guy, I followed him to a strip club. He met up with your pal Fito in the parking lot. Followed Fito here."

He asked me where my ride was, and I told him. He popped the strap on his holster and then drove down Alejandro Sandoval's street.

The Toyota was gone, as was the vehicle with the Mexican license plates. My pickup was in the same spot, appearing intact.

I got out, peered underneath, saw nothing amiss.

Throckmorton rolled down his window. "Maybe we should take a pass on this."

"Who's in the picture?" I pointed to the dash.

"Nobody you need to worry about."

Curious answer. I didn't say anything.

"Maybe we should just let this play out however it's going to play out," he said.

"Maybe not."

He stared off in the distance. Then he nodded. "OK. I'll be in touch."

• • •

I drove to the Value Rite Inn, making good time in the middle of the afternoon.

My clothes were soaked with sweat.

I had come close to killing Fito, a by-product of the anger that appeared out of nowhere, a red-hot inferno in the middle of my skull.

The idea that my rage was that powerful terrified me, made me wonder what I had become. Even worse, what would I become?

Alone in my room, I stuck a chair under the door handle and took a shower, leaving the Glock sitting on the bathroom countertop.

Hot water, lots of soap, like I was trying to wash away the filth of the city. After a few minutes, I turned the tap to cold and stood under the spray until my teeth chattered.

I dried off and got dressed, a dark-gray T-shirt, jeans, and Nikes, the Glock in my waistband.

Then I called Kiki to check on everybody. Javier was in his office doing paperwork, she told me, and Miguel was still at the movies with Torres. If it was OK, she'd like to take Miguel home for a sleepover with her kids. They would have a great time, she promised.

I didn't speak, wondering what the child-rearing books said about playdates for prepubescent assassins. Was Fito even telling the truth about Miguel?

"Arlo, are you still there?" she asked.

I told her that was fine, and we hung up. Then I called a couple of police friends, men who worked security at the Aztec Bazaar on the weekends. I asked if they could start early, like now, describing Fito and telling them that he'd been making threats against Javier and myself.

I asked the first one to position himself in the office, where Miguel would end up after the movie, the other to be out front and visible. I didn't think Fito was desperate enough to try anything in the middle of the day at a crowded place like the Aztec Bazaar, but it wouldn't hurt to have some more help. They were both off duty and agreed to head over in a few minutes.

I sat on the bed, trying to figure out my next move.

Despite appearing to be the work of a professional, the two murders were essentially street crimes. That meant the best source of information might be found on the streets.

I headed to my truck. Twenty minutes later, I drove through the parking lot of the Aztec Bazaar without stopping. The lot was about 90 percent full. Javier's pickup was in its usual place, next to my spot. One of my cop friends stood by the front door in full uniform. He waved as I went by.

Satisfied that everything was as safe as it could be, I left the parking lot.

This section of town had a significant homeless population, most of whom congregated behind a small strip center a couple of blocks away.

I drove to the strip center, parking in front of a convenience store at the end of the building. Inside the store, I bought a twelve pack of Old Milwaukee.

Ross was a good detective, and I knew that he would have tried to interview the homeless in the area, a group notoriously reluctant to talk to the police.

I wasn't a cop, not anymore at least, so I figured I might have a better chance of getting something useful. They knew me, sort of. I was the guy who let people sit under the canopy at the back of the bazaar when it rained. I bought food, too, when someone looked like they needed a hot meal, and I'd driven a couple of folks to the county hospital.

There was a small encampment on the vacant lot directly behind the convenience store. The lot was partially wooded. A couple of old storage sheds sat on the back corner. Scattered about elsewhere were a half dozen cardboard shanties.

I ambled down the alley, the beer under one arm.

Several men sat on milk cartons in the shade, smoking, drinking from cans hidden in paper bags.

One of them, a guy in his thirties wearing a filthy Dallas Cowboys sweatshirt and a porkpie hat, whistled when I got close, a warning to everybody else.

"It's all good." I held up the Old Milwaukee. "Not looking to jam anybody up."

Porkpie Hat eyed me while his two friends smoked. "What's your business here?" he asked. "We're not fond of tourists."

I put the beer on the ground a few feet in front of him. "You in charge?"

He didn't answer. One of his buddies leaned close and whispered in his ear.

"You're the guy from up the street," Porkpie Hat said. "The bazaar."

"That's right. My name is Arlo."

"What do you want, Arlo?" He reached for the twelve pack, pulled it close.

"There've been two murders in the last two days within a few blocks of here," I said. "If any of your people saw anything, I'd like to talk to them."

"My people?"

"You're in charge, aren't you?"

Most groups of homeless had an informal structure—usually a mayor to provide a semblance of leadership and a person called the sheriff to keep the peace. I had no idea if the guy in the porkpie hat was the head honcho or not, but it never hurt to stroke an ego.

"'My people' implies ownership," he said. "Everyone here is free. We take care of our own, each according to their needs and abilities. Untethered by the corporate stranglehold."

Great, I thought. *A hobo political scientist.*

"Look, Trotsky, I'd love to dialogue with you about empowering the working class, but I've got a little bit of a tick-tock situation."

"That's your paradigm, Arlo. Here, time is meaningless."

His two buddies nodded.

I pulled my wallet from my pocket and slid out a fifty-dollar bill. "Here's another constraint for you. Ulysses S. Grant. Is he meaningless, too?"

No answer. The three men stared at the money.

"I got another one just like it if you find me somebody who saw what happened."

• • •

A dining room table sat in a clearing in the middle of the vacant lot, fairly nice and in good condition, like something from a weekend sale at Nebraska Furniture Mart. Lawn chairs surrounded the table. Several men stood on the fringes of the clearing, watching me.

Porkpie Hat told me to sit at the head of the table. He disappeared behind a tree and returned a moment later with a woman in her sixties wearing a rumpled business suit. The person Miguel was afraid of.

"This is Joanie." He pulled out a seat for her to my right. "Joanie, this is Arlo."

She hesitated and then sat, glancing around nervously.

I smiled. "Hi, nice to meet you."

She licked her lips and looked to the left and then to the right, then up, then to either side again, anywhere but directly at me.

Porkpie Hat said, "Joanie has been blessed with a peculiar sense of enlightenment, one that has been poisoned by the pharmaceutical industry. Her answers may be hard to decipher."

"But she saw what happened?"

"She was nearby." He held out his hand.

I gave him another fifty and turned to the woman.

"Do you remember me?" I asked. "We've seen each other before."

"The boy," she said. "I remember him."

"Miguel."

"The boy named Miguel." She nodded. "He's not what he seems."

90

TEXAS SICARIO

The scent wafting off her was overpowering—sour onions and cheap perfume, wood smoke.

"What do you mean, Joanie?"

"He speaks to me sometimes. When you're not around."

I wondered if this was her peculiar enlightenment talking. Miguel was never away from adult supervision—Javier or me or someone else I trusted.

"At night," she said. "When I'm trying to sleep. He says terrible things to me."

"I'll ask him to stop."

"Do you want to talk about the car?" she said.

"What car?"

She frowned, lips pursed.

"Did you see a car somewhere?" I asked.

She shook her head, eyes staring down. "Never mind."

"We can talk about the car if you want."

Silence.

"OK," I said. "Let's talk about what's been going on in the neighborhood."

She closed her eyes, rocked in the chair.

"Have you heard about the murders?"

"Do you know who I am?" She opened her eyes. "Surely you do."

I shook my head.

"I am the chief comptroller for the Madison Apparel Group. I have an important meeting in a little while."

"I'll try not to keep you too long."

She crossed her arms. "Don't tell the boy about me. Please."

"Don't worry. That's our secret." I paused. "The two murders. The tire store and Mariscos. Do you know anything about either?"

"The man at the restaurant. He's nice."

"Was. He's dead."

She frowned. "He gives me food sometimes."

91

I didn't say anything.

"My meeting. I need to go."

"We'll be done in just a minute," I said. "Were you anywhere near the restaurant today?"

A long moment passed. She nodded.

"Before the police came?"

She nodded again.

"What did you see?"

"He gave me food." She wiped her eyes. "Why would someone hurt him?"

"I don't know, Joanie. There's a lot of bad people in the world." I wondered if this was going to pan out.

A reliable witness she was not. She clearly suffered from one or more mental illnesses, untreated of course, schizophrenia seeming to be at the top of the list.

She stood, agitated, and looked across the clearing. "I am trying to tell him."

I followed her gaze. She appeared to be talking to an old, doorless refrigerator.

She closed her eyes, pressed her hands against her ears. "Please. Stop yelling."

"It's OK, Joanie. Nobody's yelling."

She opened her eyes, stared at my face. "Why don't you believe me?"

"Believe what?"

"The car." She slapped the table. "The car the car the car."

The second time that topic had come up.

I kept my voice low and even. "What about the car?"

"The car killed the man who gave me food."

I took a deep breath and tried to keep my expression blank. Maybe the hundred dollars and the beer had not been a waste after all.

"What car, Joanie? Think real hard and try to remember everything you can about the vehicle you saw."

"You know what car." Her tone became lighthearted, almost silly. She waved a hand at me like we were playing a game.

"Sorry, I don't think I do."

She slapped the tabletop again. "The-car-the-car-the-car-the-car-the-car-the-car."

Porkpie Hat stepped forward, but I motioned for him to stop.

"Slow down, Joanie. Take your time. Tell me about this car."

"Miguel's car," she said. "The boy who talks to me when I'm asleep. He was in the car."

- CHAPTER SIXTEEN -

A jolt of electricity shot down my spine, circled my belly.

I jumped up, accidentally knocked over the chair. "Miguel was in the car?"

Joanie whimpered, held a hand in front of her face like she was about to be hit.

Porkpie Hat touched her shoulder, tried to be soothing. He shot me a look that said—and I'm paraphrasing here—*Are you happy now, you capitalist swine?*

I willed myself to stay calm, to concentrate on the facts, which were fairly straightforward:

One: Miguel couldn't drive.

Two: Even if he could, he didn't have access to a gun.

Three: Joanie was batshit crazy.

On the other side of the ledger was the fact that Miguel had apparently been forced to murder people for a short period, a data point that my mind refused to process in relation to what I had just learned.

"The car the car the car." She clenched her hands into fists, shoulders hunched, one side of her face twitching.

"The car." I finally understood. "With Miguel. The one he liked so much."

She nodded.

About a month ago, someone had abandoned an old Honda in the parking lot of the bazaar, a Prelude from the late nineties. The vehicle was in pristine condition, tricked out like a low-end pimpmobile—curb feelers and chrome wheels, fuzzy dice hanging from the mirror.

For reasons I would never understand, Miguel had become infatuated with that automobile, sitting behind the wheel, pretending to drive, fiddling with the controls, tapping the horn.

It was one of the few times he'd acted like a child—happy and carefree, playful—so I'd let him hang out in the Honda for most of the day, at least until Javier had someone haul the vehicle away.

Joanie must have seen him. No reason she wouldn't have. Everyone else that day had remarked on how adorable he looked behind the wheel.

I got out my phone, googled "Honda Prelude." When a picture appeared, I held the screen in front of Joanie.

"Was the car you saw at the restaurant like this one?"

She nodded.

"Did you see who was in the car?"

She shook her head. "The windows were black."

I put away the phone. That was exactly how I would have described the abandoned Honda. Windows tinted so dark that they were likely illegal.

Could Joanie have seen the same automobile at the murder scene?

Maybe but not likely. The Honda Prelude's design was hardly cutting edge, then or now. In this neighborhood, there were any number of small, inexpensive coupes that resembled such a vehicle. That was before you figured in the fact that the only witness was a mentally ill homeless person.

I continued asking questions, and she continued to answer, sometimes making sense, sometimes not.

As near as I could tell, at the time of the murder, the vehicle had been between Joanie and the owner of the seafood restaurant, the driver's side away from her. The victim turned and spoke to whoever was in the automobile. An instant later, he fell to the ground, dead.

After about fifteen minutes, Joanie's replies became less and less comprehensible. Porkpie Hat said, "We're done here. She's answered your questions."

I thought about protesting but realized it would do no good. I gave the woman one of my cards. "You've been a big help. If you need anything, come see me."

She took the card, stared at it for a moment. Then she scampered away, disappearing into the tree line.

Porkpie Hat followed me out to the alley.

"There's more money if you find any other witnesses," I said.

"I won't. Nothing good ever happens when we get mixed up in your world."

Behind him, a group of men stood in the alley, watching me with blank-bordering-on-hostile expressions on their faces, much like the people in the bar the day before.

"Thanks for your help." I headed back to my truck.

• • •

Kiki and her husband lived in northwest Dallas, near Park Lane and Webb Chapel Road, in a tract house built in the early fifties for returning servicemen buying their first home on the GI Bill.

Like much of Dallas, the area was slowly changing, older white couples selling to young Latino families.

Kiki's house was on Gaspar Drive, a tidy, one-story home with freshly painted wood siding and an enormous live oak in the front yard.

I'd called her after interviewing Joanie, asking if I could drop by and say hi to Miguel. She sounded confused at the request but told me sure, come on by.

I parked across the street.

Toys littered the yard—tricycles and bicycles, a skateboard, a half dozen balls of varying sizes and colors.

A boy a couple of years younger than Miguel answered the door, an Xbox controller in his hand.

Pandemonium inside the house—beeps and chirps from a video game, a ringing phone, a child crying, another yelling.

"Your mother here?" I asked.

He nodded and stepped aside.

Kiki appeared in the doorway leading to the kitchen, a toddler on her hip.

"C'mon in," she said. "Miguel's in the backyard."

Three boys were clustered around the TV in the living room. They were playing a game that involved zombies or werewolves or undead ninjas; it was hard to tell. They barely acknowledged my presence, jabbering with each other and working their controllers.

This was what a home felt like, a beautiful chaos, the anarchy of little angels.

A lump formed in my throat.

I pushed down the sadness and followed Kiki into the kitchen.

A pot of spaghetti sauce bubbled on the stove, filling the air with a comforting smell. In the backyard, I could see Miguel with the older children, kicking a soccer ball back and forth.

Kiki put the toddler in a playpen and looked at me. "You OK, Arlo?"

I nodded, not mentioning the run-in with Fito, instead telling her how I just wanted to see the boy, to know that he was OK.

The idea that the youngster might have been forced to kill cast his prolonged periods of silence in a new light, a glimpse of the turmoil hiding behind those innocent brown eyes.

"Miguel's having a good time," she said.

"I can see that."

"You want to stay for dinner? I could stand some adult company. Tony's got the B shift, won't be home until tomorrow morning."

Kiki's husband worked for the Dallas Fire Department, twenty-four on, forty-eight off.

"That'd be great."

She stirred the sauce. "You sure everything's OK?"

I nodded and turned away, eyes welling with tears.

"Go see Miguel," she said. "Dinner's in fifteen minutes."

I went outside, sat on a lawn chair under a willow tree.

The soccer players paid no attention to me. They ran after the ball as one large mass, yelling at each other in Spanish and English, a multiheaded organism composed of an endless series of skinny legs.

After a few minutes, the game stopped as an argument broke out over whether the ball hitting the doghouse constituted a goal or not.

Half the players lost interest and wandered away, Miguel included. He jogged over to where I was sitting.

"Hola." He plopped down cross-legged by my chair.

"How's it going?"

"That was a goal. My team should have won."

A couple of the soccer players pulled plastic guns from a basket of toys by the back door. They aimed at each other and made shooting sounds.

"Looked like a goal to me, too," I said.

We were both silent for a few moments. Miguel stared at the two boys with their plastic pistols.

"Is Javier OK?" he asked.

"Yes, he's fine."

"Are you taking me to his house?"

"No. You're spending the night with Kiki, remember?"

He nodded.

"You still want to, right?"

He nodded again, more enthusiastically.

I ruffled his hair, felt the warmth of his flesh.

Several boys tried to resurrect the soccer game. The two with the toy weapons ignored them.

"Do you remember the homeless woman who hangs around at the bazaar?" I asked. "She wears business clothes, a skirt and a blazer."

He looked up at me.

"She's kind of scary, if you ask me," I said.

He nodded. "She has crazy eyes."

An apt description.

"What about her?" he asked.

"Nothing. I saw her today is all."

Neither of us spoke for a moment.

"Someone else was killed," he said. "Did you know?"

"At the restaurant down the street."

I wondered how he had heard. News of this nature traveled fast, I supposed, like a summer grass fire.

Miguel continued to stare at the boys with the guns.

I wondered again about the missing period of his life, if it was true what Fito had said.

One of the boys dashed to where we were sitting.

He held a cap pistol in two hands, aimed at Miguel. His eyes narrowed, lips twisted into a grimace, no doubt imitating some tough guy he'd seen on TV.

Miguel stood, his hands at waist level, palms down, knees slightly bent.

I recognized the stance, the posture of someone getting ready for a fight.

"*No me apuntes con una pistola,*" Miguel said. *Don't point a gun at me.*

The boy took a step back, eyes wide. An instant later, he sprinted away, dropping the toy as he ran.

Miguel turned, and I saw his face.

He no longer looked like an eleven-year-old who'd just finished a game of soccer. His eyes were empty and cold, betraying no emotion whatsoever.

I'd seen the look before, dangerous men not bound by the usual strictures of society. Usually, when I saw that expression, I had a gun in my hand.

"It's OK," I said. "Nobody's going to hurt you."

He took a step back, breathing rapidly. He no longer looked dangerous. He looked like a lost little boy trying to find his way in a dark and scary world.

Kiki stepped out onto the back stoop and told everyone it was time to eat.

- CHAPTER SEVENTEEN -

We had a fine dinner, Kiki and the children and I.

Spaghetti and garlic bread, a salad, Popsicles for dessert. The conversation centered on video games and the latest fashion trends in athletic shoes for young adults.

When we were finished, I cleaned the kitchen while Kiki got everyone ready for bed. Then it was time for me to go.

She walked me outside in the deepening dusk, stars twinkling overhead. "Thanks for your help."

"My pleasure."

"You talked to Maria lately?"

"We had dinner last night." I decided not to elaborate.

"Good."

"Have you always wanted to be a matchmaker?" I asked.

"What are you talking about?" She raised her eyebrows, the picture of innocence.

I smiled at her.

"Maria's a nice person," she said. "So are you. What's the harm in spending time together?"

"Thanks for dinner, Kiki."

"G'night, Arlo." She waved as I got into my pickup.

I drove back to the Value Rite Motel, parked in my usual spot. Then I walked down the street to a sports bar, a place that was always full of people who seemed to be having a good time, watching whatever game was on.

I drank a couple of beers and talked to a nurse whose shift had just ended. She laughed at my jokes, even when they weren't funny. By the third time her knee accidentally rubbed against mine, I knew it was time to leave.

• • •

The next morning, a Saturday, I ate breakfast at the Denny's across the street from my motel, then headed to the bazaar.

Every weekend we hired a half dozen off-duty police officers to patrol the parking lots and walk the hallways, two of whom were the men I'd contacted the day before.

I made sure everyone was there and had a walkie-talkie with a fresh battery as well as my number on their cell.

I described Fito and told them that he had been banned from the premises for making threatening remarks toward management. If anybody saw a person fitting this description, they were to call me ASAP.

Then I headed to the office.

Javier was the only person there. He was sitting behind his desk, working through a stack of papers, a pair of reading glasses perched on his nose.

He looked up. "Miguel OK?"

"He's fine. Kiki's bringing him here after lunch."

I decided not to mention what Fito had said, about the boy being used as a hit man in South Texas. What proof did I have that his allegation was true? The way the youngster looked at me yesterday? How he reacted to a toy gun?

Instead, I told him about dinner last night, how much fun the boy seemed to be having with other children his own age.

"Why are you telling me that?" he asked.

I shrugged. "Thought you'd be interested."

"You think I don't want him to have fun?"

"I think he needs something more stable than just you and me."

"We're perfectly stable." He looked insulted.

"No, we're not," I said. "And neither of us is likely to be in the near future."

Other than the period after we first met, this was the first time either of us had mentioned our mutual suffering. We kept a lid on that aspect of our lives. We were men, after all, and men were loath to even acknowledge the existence of feelings.

"We're good people." He sniffed. "At least I am."

A weight settled on my shoulders. I felt tired, old before my time. Grief was a bitch.

"Being good doesn't mean we're doing right by the child," I said.

He rustled his papers loudly, lips pressed together. "You haven't told me anything about Fito," he said. "What do you know?"

I poured myself a cup of coffee from the pot on a side table, debating what to say.

"You're keeping something from me," he said. "The way you move, I can tell."

"Fito is a police officer from Del Rio." I didn't say anything about his connection to the DEA. No sense overloading him with bad news.

"A cop." Javier swore. "From the border."

"I think he's working for the Vaqueros."

"I knew he was a narco the first time I saw him." He shook his head. "What about you? Who are you working for now? The Texas Rangers again?"

I didn't reply, which was answer enough.

"We must keep Miguel safe," he said. "That's the important thing."

I nodded, and we were silent for a few moments. Fito wouldn't be able to get close. No way to track the boy to Kiki's, and the weekend security was on high alert to his presence.

"Do you know a homeless woman named Joanie?" I described her appearance.

"I've seen her around."

"She witnessed the second murder."

He leaned forward, excited. "What did she see?"

I told him that she didn't actually get a look at the killer, just the vehicle he or she was in, a late-nineties Honda. "A Prelude. Like the one we had towed," I said. "Whatever happened to that car?"

He drummed his fingers on the desk, brow furrowed.

After a moment, he shook his head. "I don't know."

"Let's find out, shall we?"

- CHAPTER EIGHTEEN -

Mendoza's Auto Salvage was on Davis Street, a couple of miles west of the bazaar, near Loop 12, the highway that formed an inner ring of the city.

The salvage yard was across the street from a one-story motel built in the fifties, the Players Inn, an establishment I had visited as a young state trooper when a third-string Dallas Cowboy had OD'd on a speedball—cocaine and heroin—while in the company of a transvestite prostitute named Marvelous Marla. The neighborhood looked like it had gone downhill since.

Javier directed me to the open gate facing Davis Street. An eight-foot chain-link fence topped with razor wire surrounded the entire property, maybe two acres. Except for a small office, most of the place was covered with junked automobiles and various car parts, predominately stacks of old tires as far as I could tell.

"My cousin's ex-husband," Javier said. "His uncle's brother-in-law owns the place."

"His who-what?"

"Just let me do the talking."

"Gladly." I parked by the office.

The door opened, and a Hispanic guy in greasy coveralls stepped outside.

"That's Gusano," Javier said.

"The Worm?"

"Why don't you stay in the truck while I speak to him? Gusano is affiliated with some bad people."

"How bad?"

Javier licked his lips, an apprehensive look on his face. "La Eme."

He was referring to the so-called Mexican Mafia, no relation to the Italian Cosa Nostra except for the fact that they were a full-service criminal organization, generating income from a wide variety of criminal endeavors.

Javier got out and approached the man. They bumped fists. Javier pointed to the pickup and said something. Gusano stared at me and replied without looking away. They talked for a few moments, and then Javier walked back to the passenger side of the truck.

He got in, shut the door. "Drive to the back."

A narrow path led toward the rear of the property, threading its way between rows of old cars.

"Apparently, you smell like a cop even from inside the truck," he said. "I managed to convince him that was due to your haircut, nothing else."

I pulled away from the office, Gusano still watching me, and headed down the drive.

Javier directed me to a pair of metal warehouses at the back of the yard, indicating we would be stopping at the one on the left. I parked in front of the roll-up door, and we both got out.

A heavy iron gate was between the two warehouses. I strode to the gate, which was secured by a padlock, and peered down the alley in both directions. No vehicles or people were visible.

Javier whistled. "Let's go. We don't have all day."

I walked back to the front of the warehouse.

The air smelled like old rubber and diesel fuel. This far back, the junked cars had given way to auto parts—engine blocks and wheels, transmissions and hubcaps, all stacked on open shelving.

Javier grabbed the bottom of the roll-up door and lifted it open.

The building was small, maybe fifty by fifty. One half was filled with leather seats, the third rows from various SUVs, items that were stolen so often the police maintained a separate unit dedicated to processing the insurance paperwork. Gusano was running a chop shop.

And had allowed Javier to parade a cop-smelling gringo through the middle of it. This struck me as pretty shoddy security. Or, more likely, Gusano had someone at the DPD on his payroll, and he didn't really give a damn who saw what.

Three automobiles sat in the other half of the warehouse, all of them black, vehicles that for whatever reason hadn't been stripped and sold for parts.

A late-1970s Corvette and an early 2000s Camaro, both in immaculate condition.

And the Honda Prelude that Miguel loved so much.

"Where are the keys?" I touched the hood. It was cold.

"Back in the office."

"Who has access to this building?" I could understand not chopping up the Vette and the Camaro. Not so much the Honda. Maybe Preludes were increasing in value.

"Gusano and I get along because I don't ask too many questions." Javier tried the driver's door.

It opened. He leaned in, peered around.

"Don't touch anything," I said. "I've got gloves in the truck."

He ignored me, stuck his head in the back seat.

I wanted to call Throckmorton, get a team here to dust for prints. Even as I thought about making the call, I realized the futility. Probable cause for a legitimate search was thin to nonexistent, the testimony of a mentally ill homeless person. Not to mention getting someone out here to print the car would cause Gusano to make a big frowny face.

Javier extricated himself from the rear of the vehicle. In one hand, he held a tiny green football, a promotional item for a check-cashing business inside the bazaar.

"This is Miguel's. Remember? He must have left it in here while he was playing."

The youngster loved that silly little green ball almost as much as he loved the abandoned Honda. When the football had turned up missing, he'd searched for days and days.

I crouched by the open front door and peered in the car.

The inside of the vehicle was just as I remembered. Clean and well cared for, the dash shiny from a spray-on protectant. The same fuzzy dice dangled from the rearview mirror, the expensive stereo still in place.

I walked to the other side. Using my shirttail, I opened the passenger door and examined the floor and seat, a likely place to find a spent cartridge if the shooter fired out the passenger window.

No shiny metal objects were visible.

I looked under the seat, then in the back, saw nothing.

I shut the door. "Hate to ask, seeing as how Gusano is your cousin's uncle's life partner or whatever, but do you think he could be involved in Sandoval's murder?"

"I do not like the man, and I certainly think he has it in his heart to kill." Javier paused. "But I don't think he is responsible for the murders."

I waited, figuring there had to be more.

"The cars," Javier said. "He has a nice business. Why would he want to endanger that?"

A good point. That didn't mean he wasn't doing subcontractor work for one of the other cartels, but it lessened the odds because he didn't need the money.

"I could be wrong," he said. *"No sería la primera vez."*

I pointed to the other warehouse. "What's in there?"

"Things we should not ask about."

I could only imagine—pneumatic tools and heavy-duty jacks, hydraulic lifts, everything needed to strip a car down to its chassis.

The odds were slim that this Honda had been involved in the murders. But it was a base that needed to be covered, a box to check. That was the way an investigation worked. You ran everything to ground, no matter how far-fetched. What remained was the answer. Usually.

Before I could say anything else, a late-model Ford pickup appeared from the front, driving slowly between the stacks of auto parts.

Gusano was in the passenger seat. A heavyset man with a ponytail sat behind the wheel.

The pickup stopped in front of the second warehouse, and Gusano got out. He ambled over to where Javier and I were standing.

"Are you finished?" Gusano asked.

Javier nodded. "*Gracias.* We'll be leaving now."

Gusano stared at me, eyes unblinking and hostile.

"The Honda," I said. "Has it been here ever since you towed it from the bazaar?"

Javier took a sharp breath, cut his eyes my way.

Gusano continued to stare at me, a challenge. After a long moment, he said, "I'm doing a favor for Javier. He wanted to see the car. You don't get to ask questions."

"Can I take that as a no?"

Sometimes you had to check the boxes extra hard, just to be sure. Kick up a little dust.

Javier moved toward the passenger door of my truck. "It's time for us to leave, Arlo."

"In a minute," I said. "The Worm is getting ready to answer."

Gusano balled his fists, nostrils flaring as he took several angry breaths. He bounced on the balls of his feet, moving in my direction, obviously wanting to give me a beatdown.

"Don't even think about it." I shook my head. "I promise it won't end well for you."

He stopped. After a moment, he looked at Javier. "You bring a cop here? What have I ever done to you?"

The driver's door of the Ford opened, and the guy with the ponytail got out. He was nearly as big as the Honda, tattoos like sleeves on his arms.

"For the record, I'm an ex-cop," I said. "And it's a simple question. Has the Honda left the premises since you towed it here?"

Ponytail lumbered over. "Everything cool?"

I stared at Gusano. "The next people who come asking about that car, they'll have badges and warrants."

Ponytail frowned. "What the hell is he talking about?"

"The auto theft unit'll be first," I said. "Then the DEA."

Ponytail backed away, eyes wide.

Gusano shot a rage-filled glance at Javier. "The car's not left here."

"Not a single time?" I said. "Not since you've had it?"

He shook his head once. Then he pointed toward the exit. "Get the hell off my property."

I strolled back to my truck, got inside, cranked the ignition.

Javier stared out the window, an angry silence coming off him like a fever.

I turned the pickup around, headed toward the street.

He said, "You miss it, don't you? Being a cop. Fucking with people."

I sped up.

"I've never seen you act like that."

"Like what?" I pulled onto Davis.

"Like an asshole."

"People are being killed."

"Gusano is not someone you want as an enemy," he said.

"Neither are the Vaqueros."

We rode the rest of the way to the Aztec Bazaar without speaking.

- CHAPTER NINETEEN -

Javier told me to drop him off at the bar.

"You planning to tie one on?" I asked.

Sullen silence.

I pulled in to the parking lot, headed toward the front of El Corazón Roto. Before the vehicle came to a complete stop, he jumped out.

"Take care of Miguel." He slammed the pickup's door and disappeared inside.

I idled for a moment, watching the front of the bar. A car behind me honked, and I reluctantly headed to my parking space on the other side of the building.

It was a busy day at the Aztec Bazaar. I took up my usual position by the front, a stool with a low back, just past the statue of Our Lady of Guadalupe, a perch that offered a good view of people as they entered and exited.

By text and walkie-talkie, I checked in with the weekend security crew.

Nothing was amiss, aside from the usual problems that came with crowds of people. Fender benders and lost keys, children who'd wandered off, misplaced purses. No sign of anyone who resembled Fito.

I hoped that was a good omen. Maybe he was off *investigating* one of the other murders, forgetting about us for the moment.

Maybe he'd stay gone, and we could get back to normal, whatever that was, two grief-stricken men, one prone to excessive drinking, trying to take care of an orphan who had no legal standing in this country. Maybe pigs could operate submarines, too.

While I sat there, I pulled out the list Throckmorton had given me and scanned the contents, searching for some hidden significance that had eluded me before.

But there was nothing. Just names. Some dead, some still alive, presumably.

The name after Juan Gonzalez, Pecky Ruibal, was unusual enough that it might lead to something during an internet search.

I pulled out my phone as Maria sauntered by. She smiled but didn't stop, which was OK because I didn't feel like talking right then.

I had just tapped out "Pecky" when Miguel burst through the front entrance, zigzagging his way through the shoppers, skidding to a stop by my stool. Kiki was right behind him, a bemused look on her face.

"Arlo." The boy tugged on my jeans, his face animated. "The zoo, Arlo. *The zoo.*"

I put my phone away and slid off the barstool. "Slow down. What are you talking about?"

"Kiki." He was almost hyperventilating. "She—The zoo—Today—"

After a few moments, I pieced together what he was trying to tell me. Kiki and her kids had free tickets to an event at the zoo that afternoon. Would it be OK if Miguel went?

He was more excited than I had ever seen him. A deep smile curled across his face, eyes animated with the prospect of seeing all the animals.

I wondered how a boy with a smile like that could be a killer. Then I remembered his face in Kiki's backyard when the kid with the toy gun had approached him.

Kiki asked if Miguel could spend another night with her family. Her husband, Tony, would be off work, and after the zoo they all planned to go to Chuck E. Cheese's for pizza.

I told her of course he could go, and while I didn't want to impose, if she and her family wanted him to spend the night again, that was OK as well.

Miguel hopped from foot to foot, ecstatic at the news.

Kiki smiled, happy as well. After a moment, she said, "You think it's OK with Javier? I don't want to, well, you know."

She glanced in the direction of El Corazón Roto, an almost involuntary movement.

"It'll be fine," I said, not telling her that Javier had probably crawled into a bottle of bourbon, and the youngster certainly didn't need to be around that.

I gave Miguel a ten-dollar bill. "Go get something for Kiki's kids, a present for being so nice."

He scampered toward a store that sold Mexican candies. When he was out of earshot, Kiki said, "He's a good boy. A pleasure to be around."

I stared down the hall where he'd gone, remembering my own son.

"Javier." She paused. "He worries me sometimes."

I came back to the present.

"The drinking," she said. "You know what I mean, right?"

I nodded.

"Miguel is very attached to him. And you, too, of course."

I waited, sensing there was a point to the conversation.

"If it comes down to it," she said. "You need to be the one who takes charge of things for Miguel."

I looked back down the hall. We were both silent for a moment.

"Does he ever talk about his life before Dallas?" I asked.

She shook her head.

"I wonder what that was like," I said. "Just how bad it was."

A moment passed.

"What's going to happen, Arlo? Are you going to adopt Miguel or what?"

I was living in a pay-by-the-week motel. What kind of environment would that be for a kid? Even if I had a house with a white picket fence and a loving wife, would I be able to provide proper care for someone who'd been through what Miguel had endured?

Would anybody?

"He doesn't have papers. There's nothing to adopt," I said. "And we don't want to get the courts involved, obviously."

Kiki nodded. She'd been born in this country, but her parents had been illegal. While she loved America, she had a healthy distrust of the authorities.

"What about when he gets older?" she said. "What then?"

"I don't know." I tried not to sound as frustrated as I felt. "We just take it one day at a time."

She stared at the throngs of shoppers filling the halls. "It's so sad. I wonder if anyone will ever come looking for him."

I'd been pondering that same question, asking myself if maybe they already had.

• • •

Kiki and Miguel left for the zoo, and I returned to Google.

There were two Pecky Ruibals in the Dallas area. One was a retired plumber in his eighties, the other an accordion player in a conjunto band, Los Tres Reyes, The Three Kings, a group that frequently toured throughout Texas, especially the southern half.

Pecky the musician was in his thirties and had an active social media presence, specifically Twitter and Instagram accounts, both of which were filled with pictures of Pecky and his fans, mostly raven-haired beauties and guys who dressed like Juarez street thugs.

He also had a web page, which was where I found his email address.

I looked through the band's schedule of past gigs and then dropped Pecky a note, saying that I was a screenwriter who had recently caught his show in Austin, and I'd be interested in talking to him about a script I was working on. I left my cell number.

Two hours later, I was drinking a cup of coffee from my perch by the front door, watching people come and go, when my phone rang, a number I didn't recognize.

I answered.

Quinn Vega's voice on the other end, frantic. "Arlo. Please help."

I jumped off the barstool. "What's wrong?"

No answer.

"Quinn, are you OK?"

No noise from the other end except what sounded like the *ding-ding* of a car door left open.

"Quinn?"

"Frank," she said. "Someone's trying to kill him."

- CHAPTER TWENTY -

Dallas wasn't known for its intrinsic beauty, unless you were into prairie land and dry creek beds. Still, there were parts of the city that possessed a certain natural charm. One of those was the area around White Rock Lake, a large man-made body of water in the eastern half of town.

The Vegas' house was on Fisher Road, on a small rise that offered a nice view of the water. The lot was small for the area, about a half acre or a little larger, partially wooded.

The front gate was open, so I drove up a gravel driveway and stopped behind the Maserati, which was parked at an angle like whoever had driven the car last had been in a hurry to get out.

The vehicle sat in front of a large one-story home made from cream-colored stone, topped with a tin roof. A detached three-car garage was behind the house at the edge of the property, underneath a live oak that looked like it had been planted during the Coolidge administration.

Quinn Vega opened the front door of the house before I could get out of my pickup. She was wearing Nike trainers, a pair of yoga pants that came to just below her knees, and a sleeveless workout shirt.

Saturday attire for people who paid to have their houses cleaned and their dogs walked.

She strode toward me, obviously worried.

Frank Vega appeared in the entryway. He wore a dark slim-fit suit with a white dress shirt, no tie. Saturday attire for hipster undertakers or criminal defense attorneys who might need to appear before a judge at any moment.

He just stood there, shaking his head, not really inside the house or out. Like he couldn't decide which way to go.

"Thank you for coming," Quinn said.

"What happened?"

She glanced at her husband, about twenty feet away.

"Why'd you get him involved?" Frank called out.

Quinn touched my arm, her fingers cool and dry. "I'm scared, Arlo."

"Somebody try to break in?"

Frank Vega stepped outside, slammed the door. "This is ridiculous."

"How can you say that?" Quinn faced her husband, voice choked with emotion.

I waited.

After a moment, Frank sighed loudly, clearly exasperated. "Fine. I'll show you."

He marched toward the garage.

I followed, Quinn a step behind me.

All three doors were open.

In the far right slot was a Mercedes sedan. Boxes and discarded exercise equipment filled the far left. The middle space was empty.

Frank grasped the cord at the bottom of the middle door, his fingers barely able to reach. He pulled down.

The door was wooden, painted a flat white. Unremarkable except for two crude figures spray-painted in black, a skull next to a sickle.

Beneath the figures was a phrase: *"Plomo para mis enemigos."*

"Lead for my enemies." Quinn pointed to the words. "That sounds like a threat to me."

I looked at Frank. "I take it you're the enemy?"

He didn't reply.

"Any idea what this is about?" I could still smell the paint. Whoever had defaced the door had done so within the past hour or so.

"My line of work," he said, "you occasionally come into contact with some unpleasant people."

Almost exactly the same thing that his wife had said yesterday.

"You mean your clients?"

"Everyone deserves zealous representation." He crossed his arms, his words sounding like a brochure for the bar association.

"Any client in particular come to mind?"

Frank didn't answer. Instead he glanced at his wife and then turned away from both of us, staring at the door.

"When did you first notice this?" I asked.

"I had a brunch meeting," he said. "It wasn't there when I left."

"What time was that?"

He continued to stare at the garage door, appearing lost in thought.

"Ten o'clock," Quinn said. "That's when he left this morning."

For a brunch meeting. On Saturday. I didn't say anything.

Frank looked away from the door and scowled at me, chin jutting out, angry for no apparent reason.

"Then what happened?" I asked.

"He came back about twenty minutes ago, and we both saw it," Quinn said. "That's when I called you."

"So were you here when it happened?"

"Yes." She paused. "Alone."

They glared at each other, waves of anger rippling between them.

"Did you hear or see anything?" I asked.

She shook her head.

"What about video? Any cameras on the property?"

"Some people have a different way of communicating than you and I do," Frank said. "Let's not blow this out of proportion."

"This isn't communicating, Frank. This is a threat." Quinn turned to me. "We have cameras on the doors to the house and part of the backyard. Nothing on the garage."

The garage appeared to be accessible only from the front of the property, the gravel drive I had used.

An ivy-covered masonry wall, about eight feet tall, surrounded the entire lot. After a moment, I noticed a small wrought iron gate near the left side of the garage, closest to the space filled with boxes.

I walked to the gate, knelt so that I was eye level with the latching mechanism.

A push-button keypad lock secured the entry. Punch in a four-digit code from either side and you could come and go as you pleased.

Up close, I could see that the lock was shattered. Pieces lay on the gravel drive, sprayed out like something had impacted the mechanism from the street side.

Something like a bullet.

I looked across the driveway, trying to guess where a round would have hit.

The house was about fifty feet away, shaded by a pair of magnolias more or less in a direct line of sight from the damaged lock.

Maybe we'd get lucky and find the bullet. Maybe not. That was a job for the police. I imagined that getting them involved was going to be an issue with Frank Vega.

I used my shirttail to grab a rung and opened the gate.

"That's supposed to be locked," Frank said.

"Yeah. I can see that. Somebody shot it, though."

Quinn gasped as I stepped outside and peered in either direction.

Live oaks and elms lined both sides of Fisher Road, shading the surface of the street. There were no cars or people visible.

I walked a few yards toward the lake, trying to get a feel for what the perp had seen, how he might have acted, where he would have parked.

Through a break in the trees, I could see a sailboat slice across the surface of the lake, the water like glass. This was a pleasant neighborhood, the residents not ready for the violence they read about in the Sunday papers encroaching on their bucolic section of Dallas.

Quinn appeared beside me.

"You need to call the police," I said, keeping my voice low.

"Frank won't like that." She looked back toward the gate, clearly nervous.

"This isn't about what he likes or doesn't like. This is about not getting killed."

"You don't understand," she whispered.

I continued to stare at the water, wondering who had cameras in the area, which direction the person responsible would have come from.

A moment passed.

"What are you two talking about?" Vega stood in the entryway to his property.

I turned away from the lake. "Who's the client?"

"Does it really matter?" He crossed his arms.

I waited for him to continue.

"You have any idea who these people are?" he asked. "The resources they possess?"

Two people had been murdered, the ones of which I had direct knowledge. According to Throckmorton, there'd been others, and there were more to come.

I wondered if there was another list, one with Frank Vega's name on it. I couldn't see a direct connection between the two killings and the defaced garage door. But I'd been a law enforcement officer for too many years not to grasp that there had to be a link.

Whatever the connection was, the killer needed to be caught. That was my baseline, the cop in me, even before I considered the veiled threats to Miguel.

"You can't stop them," he said. "No one can."

"Stop who?" I asked.

Silence.

Quinn said, "Tell him, Frank."

No response.

"Either of you know a man named Fito Alvarez?" I asked.

Quinn closed her eyes. She reached a hand out to steady herself on the brick wall that surrounded her home.

Frank Vega said, "We'd better go inside so I can explain."

- CHAPTER TWENTY-ONE -

The interior of the Vega home was straight out of *Architectural Digest*, the Scandinavian edition, all marble and chrome and abstract art, expensive but cold.

Frank led me to a large sitting area. A thirty-foot-wide picture window served as the far wall, offering a view of the lake. The opposite wall was dominated by a series of artworks that looked like a four-year-old had thrown paint at the canvas until it was nap time.

"Would you like a drink?" Frank stood by a bar in the corner.

I shook my head.

Quinn sat on a low-slung leather sofa, legs folded underneath her.

Frank poured himself a couple of ounces of whiskey. Glass in hand, he walked across the room to the window and stared out at the lake.

I sat on the other side of the sofa, opposite Quinn.

"Pax was his name." Frank took a sip of his drink. "Pax Larson-Ibarra, which is a funny name for a Mexican when you think about it."

While his wife shivered in the air-conditioning, Frank Vega told me the story of how he came to be involved with the most dangerous criminal organization in the hemisphere.

• • •

Frank operated as a solo practitioner, lots of drop-in business. He maintained an office in a converted house in the Uptown section of Dallas, a tony neighborhood frequented by well-heeled millennials who sometimes forgot to take Uber when they'd had too much to drink or neglected to get rid of the edibles from their last trip to Colorado.

He liked working by himself. He didn't have to answer to anyone, attend any partner meetings. He had no pressure to up his billable hours.

The solo part had a flip side, however. He was the only one generating any income. Which was fine so long as the work was steady and the rents from his small real estate portfolio kept pace with the expenses and the mortgage payments.

But if his caseload ever slowed and the local property market took a nosedive, then the problems started.

Problems such as the registered letter he'd recently received from the bank that held the note on several of his largest properties. Frank had missed three payments, resulting in a default and an official demand for remedy. The letter contained phrases like "post for foreclosure" and "your personal guarantee of the loan," words that brought a chill to Frank's skin.

He was reading that letter for the third time when a call came in from a longtime client, a man who owned a bus company specializing in routes to and from Dallas and various border towns. The client had referred a friend, a Mexican national from a rural area in the state of Coahuila, to the Law Offices of Frank Vega, P.C.

Pax Larson-Ibarra and his family owned a number of Laundromats and pawnshops in South Texas as well as several ranches in Mexico. He had recently asked Frank's client for the name of a good attorney—not somebody at a big firm, too much overhead and bureaucracy, but someone qualified to handle a criminal case. Naturally, the bus company owner had thought of Frank. *Take care of Pax,* he said. *He's good people.*

The next day, Pax arrived at Frank's office. The man was in his late thirties and clearly well off, as evidenced by his clothes, tailored khakis and a navy-blue polo shirt, the iconic Ralph Lauren insignia oversize, the way rich people south of the border preferred. Then there was the watch, a gold Rolex, the Presidential model.

As they made small talk, Frank tried to guess what Pax's problem was, figuring perhaps the man had consumed too many glasses of wine at one of Dallas's many fine restaurants and been pulled over by the police.

If it were a first offense, well, Frank was friends with most of the prosecutors at the DA's office, and surely something could be worked out.

Pax shook his head at the mention of driving under the influence. "My nephew. He made a mistake, trusted the wrong people."

Frank nodded sympathetically, wondering if it was a controlled substance issue.

Ever since Colorado had legalized cannabis, people had been trying to bring back small quantities of the drug, tiny bud-filled vials with innocuous names like Mango Kush or Cherry Pie. Innocuous, at least until the Texas authorities found out.

Pax looked at Frank's diploma on the wall, a Juris Doctor from Baylor University, the best school in the state if you wanted to ply your trade in a Texas courtroom.

"My nephew, he was apprehended with a quantity of marijuana in his possession."

Frank allowed himself a tiny moment of pleasure that he had guessed correctly. He jotted down some notes on a yellow pad. Then he wrote, RETAINER??

"The Dallas police," Pax said. "They pulled him over in Oak Cliff."

"How much did he have in his possession?"

Pax hesitated, clearly embarrassed. "He's a good boy. You understand that?"

"I do, of course. Good people get in trouble all the time," Frank said. "That's one reason lawyers stay in business."

"The police." Pax sighed. "They can be so unreasonable."

Frank clucked his tongue sympathetically and waited.

"Seven kilos," Pax said. "How much is that? Fourteen, fifteen pounds?"

A lot, that's how much it is, Frank thought. Not just a few gummy bears from a dispensary in Denver or a vape pen loaded with a couple of grams of hash.

Fifteen pounds represented serious time. Also, a serious retainer.

"Tell me about your fee structure," Pax said.

Frank glanced at the man's watch and clothes, the perfectly styled hair. He mentioned a number, double his usual retainer.

Pax nodded. "Will cash be OK?"

Frank licked his lips but didn't reply.

Over the years, clients had paid in a variety of ways—guns, real estate, automobiles, livestock, and of course cash. But those had all been people with whom Frank had a prior relationship. Not a cold referral.

"You're worried about the IRS form, aren't you?" Pax said.

Frank hesitated and then nodded sheepishly.

The Internal Revenue Service required any business accepting more than $10,000 for a good or service to file a Form 8300, detailing the amount of cash received and the identity of the payer, Social Security number, DOB, etc.

"I'm happy to fill one out," Pax said.

"Wonderful." Frank smiled. "Not that I mind the cash, but I like to keep Uncle Sam happy."

"Of course." Pax stood. "Do you mind if I get the money now?"

Frank nodded, feeling relieved, and printed off the proper form from the IRS's website while Pax went outside. Two minutes later, his new client returned and placed a leather briefcase on Frank's desk. He opened the case, displaying stacks of $100 bills.

Frank stared at the currency for a few seconds, prioritizing where the money should go, what hole in his leaking ship he should plug first. Then he handed Pax the government form and took the cash to a small safe in his storeroom. When he returned, Pax gave him back the slip of paper.

"The name on there," he said. "That's my brother. The money comes from him."

The elation Frank felt at his sudden windfall turned sour.

"It's supposed to be your name." He looked at Pax. "That's the rule."

"But the money's not mine."

Frank scanned the form again, squinting at the address for the brother, what looked like a PO Box in San Antonio.

"Is this going to be a problem?" Pax said.

Before Frank could reply, his cell phone rang, the caller ID indicating it was the credit card company trying to reach him. He sent the call to voice mail and looked at the IRS form again.

"I like you, Frank. And our mutual friend speaks very highly of your skills." Pax smiled. "But there are other lawyers in Dallas."

Frank made his decision. He stuck the form in his desk drawer and said, "I just need the paperwork. Now let's talk about the case."

They discussed the specifics for a few minutes and then made an appointment to get together the following day with Pax's nephew.

• • •

A month later, Frank was preparing for the first court date when Pax and the nephew, a young man in his early twenties who wore silk shirts and pointy-toed cowboy boots, dropped by to make another payment, also in cash.

"That's not necessary," Frank said. "I'll let you know when the retainer is gone."

"You're going to need the money anyway." Pax shrugged. "Why not take it now?"

This is true, Frank acknowledged to himself. The case against the nephew would be difficult to win. Despite repeated requests, the friend who actually owned the marijuana was never made available to Frank, so he had to go with the narrative summed up in the police report—a story the accused did little to contradict.

Pax's nephew had been alone when he was pulled over, driving in a car with a broken taillight. The police had probable cause to search his vehicle because the idiot was smoking a joint at the time. On the rear floorboard, in a bag of laundry the nephew was supposed to be dropping off at the friend's house, they had found a plastic-wrapped package of marijuana.

Frank had several strategies for mounting a credible defense, but in the end, he knew that a plea deal was the best option for the young man. Pax, however, was vehemently opposed to the idea. His nephew had been doing a favor for a friend; why should he have his name besmirched?

"Money for a good defense is not a problem," Pax said. "Do the best you can."

Frank shrugged and accepted the second briefcase full of cash, and the ones that followed in the subsequent weeks. After each payment, Pax filled out the proper paperwork using his brother's name.

Finally, the day after the sixth payment, Frank received a phone call from the prosecutor. The case was being dismissed, a problem with the only witness, the arresting officer. The prosecutor was tight-lipped, no further details forthcoming, though she obviously sounded displeased.

Frank called Pax with the good news and listened to the two men sing his praises as he thought about all the money he would have to refund.

Pax seemed to read his thoughts. "You've done such a good job for us," he told Frank. "Why don't you just refund a portion, say fifty percent."

Frank hesitated; the amount he'd keep was too much for the work he'd done. After a moment, he reluctantly agreed, seeing as how half of what he'd been paid would be just enough to keep things going until he got some more business. The next day, after receiving instructions from Pax, he wired the money to the brother's account at a bank in Matamoros, not in San Antonio.

Frank was glad to have the influx of capital, but truth be told, he was more glad to be rid of Pax. The brother's info on the IRS form, the Mexican bank, the slimy nephew—nothing about the situation felt right to Frank.

A week later, Pax dropped by unannounced.

Another relative had been arrested, this one in Fort Worth.

Pax held up a briefcase, wordlessly asking if Frank would be open to representing another family member.

Frank realized that he was being used to launder money. On some level, he'd probably known all along, but the cash was tantalizing, as it was meant to be.

He took a deep breath and looked Pax in the eye. "I don't think so. Not this time."

Pax cocked his head. "You're turning me down?"

"That's correct."

Pax sighed the way a parent does when a child won't clean his room.

"I hope you understand," Frank said. "My caseload is very full right now."

No one spoke for a few moments.

Pax stared out the window, a wistful look on his face. "There's a man coming in from out of town. If you don't mind, he'd like to talk to you about your decision."

"Uh, who is he?" Frank tried not to sound concerned at this new bit of information.

"He works for my family," Pax said. "His name is Fito."

● ● ●

Frank had finished his drink. He stood by the window that looked out over the lake, holding the empty glass, staring into the bottom.

I glanced at Quinn, still on the other side of the couch.

She'd tucked her knees under her chin, arms wrapped around her legs, body language speaking volumes about what she was no doubt feeling.

"Tell me about Fito," I said. "Finish the story."

Quinn got off the couch, padded to the bar. She poured herself a glass of white wine, drank half of it in one gulp.

"A couple years ago, I defended a serial killer." Frank mentioned the name of a man who'd cut out the tongues of women he met on a dating website. "He got stabbed in lockup and died before we went to trial, which I wasn't unhappy about."

I waited.

"He was the scariest person I'd ever encountered." Frank paused. "Until I met Fito."

Quinn spoke for the first time since we'd gone inside. "He showed us videos."

"Videos?" I said.

She twirled a lock of hair between her thumb and forefinger, a faraway look on her face. "What they do to people. I didn't know that level of . . . of . . . evil was possible."

She didn't need to go into detail. I'd heard the stories; anyone in law enforcement had. The stuff of nightmares, humankind's ability to be inhuman, hard to get your head around.

"So what happened?" I asked.

"We did what he wanted," Frank said. "What else could we do?"

An understandable position. Because even if he ran to the authorities and managed to escape Fito's wrath, there was still the matter of the crimes Frank Vega had committed, the money laundering and accepting what had to be a falsified IRS form.

"How do you know about Fito?" Quinn asked.

"He showed up at the Aztec Bazaar two days ago."

Frank shook his head like he wasn't surprised at the news.

"Pax," I said. "Tell me about him. What did he look like?"

"Average, a little less than six feet, weight proportionate," Frank said. "Except for his face. He had a birthmark on one cheek, a splotch like someone had spilled a glass of wine."

I recognized the description.

The guy in the Sandovals' backyard.

- CHAPTER TWENTY-TWO -

Quinn downed the last of her wine. She picked up the bottle, started to pour a second glass.

"Another one?" Frank said.

She ignored him and filled the glass up to a spot just below the rim. "Not today, Frank. Don't nitpick me to death today."

Her husband swore and slammed his empty highball on the bar.

"You want me to wait outside?" I sensed that all was not well in the Vega marriage, above and beyond being under the thumb of a drug cartel.

No answer.

Quinn took a gulp of Chardonnay. Her face was pale, arms stubbled with gooseflesh.

"Back to the matter at hand," I said. "You need to call the DEA."

Frank's eyes grew wide. "You say that after what I just told you?"

"That's your best worst option," I said. He'd have to take his lumps in regard to the money he'd accepted, the crimes already committed. But bringing in the feds represented the highest probability of staying alive.

"It's just some spray paint," Frank said. "Don't rock the boat. That's all they're saying."

Quinn drained the second glass of wine, reached for the bottle again.

"That's enough." Frank shook his head, angry.

"Screw you." She poured a third glass.

I got off the sofa and ambled to the bar. I slid my fingers around the glass in her hand and gently pulled it from her grasp.

She didn't resist.

I put the wine down next to the bottle. "You need to keep a clear head."

No reply.

"Do you have somewhere to go?" I asked Frank. "A friend's house or a family member?"

He shook his head. "We're not running."

I looked at Quinn. "What about you? Anybody you can stay with for a few days?"

She crossed her arms. "I can't take this to someone else's doorstep."

I had no answer to that. I turned to her husband. "The spray paint. Why now? Have you been rocking the boat?"

"Not me," he said. "But the ship's in rough waters at the moment."

I waited for him to continue.

"People who work for the organization have been murdered," he said. "Sandoval and the other guy, the one at the restaurant."

"Along with a man in Hillsboro," I said. "And several others."

"How do you know about that?" He stared at me, brow furrowed.

"I used to be a cop. That was my job, knowing stuff."

"Then you understand that these killings impact their business," he said. "Especially since they're just getting established in this part of the world."

"What did they do?" I asked. "Sandoval and the restaurant guy?"

"The organization uses automobiles to transport their product. Sandoval's business was a tire store."

I nodded, understanding the implications. There were dozens of places in a vehicle to hide contraband. A tire store would be an ideal place to handle the shipments.

"And the restaurant has a lot of freezer space," he said. "Perfect for storage."

"Do you have any idea who might have killed those men?"

"Do I look like a homicide detective?" He was back to sounding pompous and arrogant.

"No. That's one of Fito's jobs, from what I hear," I said.

Quinn flinched at the mention of the man's name.

"Investigations for the Vaqueros," I continued.

"You know an awful lot about the organization." Frank stared at me. "Makes me wonder whose side you're on."

"If you're worried about me, I can leave."

Quinn shook her head. "Please don't."

I debated asking Frank about the other names on the list. Maybe he had an idea who they were, a way to reach each man, to warn them.

Before I could say anything, he looked at his watch. "I have to go."

Quinn shook her head, lips curled into a sneer of disgust. She plopped down on the sofa and stared outside.

"Now?" I said.

"I have an appointment." He opened a cabinet on the bar and removed a small pistol, what looked like a .380-caliber semiautomatic.

"What are you doing with that?" I asked.

"Protecting myself." He stuck the weapon in his back pocket.

"Frank and his guns," Quinn said. "Almost like he's overcompensating for something."

He flexed his fingers and glared at his wife, lips pressed together.

"You know how to use that thing?" I asked.

"I have a concealed-carry permit. It's perfectly legal."

"Good for you. But do you know how to use it?"

The Vaqueros armed themselves with fully automatic rifles, military-grade weapons firing rounds capable of piercing cinder block walls. Frank's pistol was a mouse gun, barely able to puncture a two-by-four.

He ignored my question. He pulled a tin of mints from his pocket, popped one in his mouth. "I'll call a painter. We'll get that mess on the garage door cleaned up."

Quinn glanced at me, eyes fearful. A painter wasn't going to fix this.

Frank spoke to his wife. "I'll be home late. Don't wait up."

Then he was gone from the room. A moment later, I heard the throaty rumble of his Maserati. A few seconds later, that disappeared, too.

I walked to the front door, made sure it was locked. Back in the living room, Quinn was still on the sofa, staring outside.

"Do you know where he's going right now?" she asked.

I didn't say anything.

"He has a meeting with a state senator. After that, he's taking his mistress to dinner."

"Very European. The mistress part anyway."

She didn't speak.

"You and Frank been married long?" I asked.

"Ten years. Second time for both of us."

I glanced around the room, wondering about children. I had trouble envisioning kids romping through the Vega ice palace.

"What am I supposed to do now?" she asked. "I can't stay here, that's for sure."

I told her about my motel. "They have rooms available. You can use a different name, pay in cash."

She didn't say anything. I could only imagine what was running through her mind, going from an estate overlooking the water to a pay-by-the-week motel in a sketchy part of town.

Such was life when you were in bed with a gang of violent criminals.

"None of my business," I said. "But why do you two stay together?"

"You want me to tell you about the sanctity of the marriage vows? Or maybe you'd like to hear how Frank's a good man who makes bad choices?"

The room darkened as clouds gathered outside. This time of the summer, pop-up thunderstorms were a common occurrence in the late afternoon.

Her lips set themselves into a hard line, eyes flinty and hard.

"You ever been poor, Arlo?"

My parents had been college professors. We were comfortable, but wealth was never part of our existence. I remembered the story about Quinn's father losing his money, almost going to jail. A fast and hard fall.

"Give me ten minutes." She stood and left the room.

- CHAPTER TWENTY-THREE -

Quinn Vega had been gone nine and a half minutes when my cell phone rang, a local number that was unfamiliar.

I was in Frank's office, a room just off the sitting area that was paneled in dark wood and decorated with overstuffed leather chairs like an English gentlemen's club.

I answered. "Arlo Baines."

Ross's voice on the other end. "I think maybe it's time you come downtown so we can have a little chitchat."

I waited for him to say more, admiring the zebra-skin rug below my feet.

"When did you become a screenwriter?" he asked. "That actually makes me laugh."

The email I'd sent earlier to Pecky Ruibal, the guy in the band that toured throughout Texas. The implications of how Ross knew about my message gave me a chill.

Across the lake, a cloud bank as dark as midnight flashed white. The light reflected off the heavy glass doors of a gun cabinet on one wall. A moment later, thunder rattled the windows.

"What are you talking about?" I asked.

"You tell me."

Quinn came into the room, a leather duffel bag over one shoulder. She'd showered and changed. Her hair was wet, pulled back into a pony-tail. She was wearing a pair of jeans and a black blouse, sleeveless, snug on her torso.

"I don't have time for this, Ross. You got something to say, say it."

A whistling noise on the other end like wind was blowing while he walked.

"I've got another body," he said. "And an email from a guy named Arlo Baines on the stiff's phone."

So that had been the right Pecky, and now he was dead.

"Where are you?" I asked.

A moment passed. I could almost hear him thinking, wondering what to say next, how far to push me. He knew the odds were better that he'd win the lottery than get me into a police station voluntarily.

"You ever hear of a place called El Club de la Paloma?" He gave me an address south of White Rock Lake, a commercial area near the interstate.

Raindrops fluttered against the window.

"On my way." I ended the call.

•   •   •

El Club de la Paloma, The Dove Club in English, was in an old PetSmart on Garland Road, next to a muffler shop and a place that sold discount tobacco products.

Clouds filled the sky, purple and heavy. Thunder rumbled in the distance. Despite the smattering of rain back at Quinn's house, the storm hadn't started yet.

The parking lot at The Dove Club was empty except for police cars—more than at the other crime scenes—and a tour bus, gleaming and black, the words **LOS TRES REYES** emblazoned on the side.

Two Hispanic men milled around the front of the bus, members of the band or roadies. They were talking to several police officers, pointing to the club.

Yellow tape segmented off an area on one side of the building.

Quinn and I were in my truck. I drove toward the tape and parked by an unmarked squad car.

"Stay here. You'll be safe with all these cops around." I exited the pickup.

The air felt heavy with the threat of rain. Wind whipped across the parking lot, blowing dirt and trash.

Ross met me where the tape was attached to the side of the building, a pair of uniformed officers behind him. He squinted at my vehicle.

"Who's that?" he said. "You on a date or what?"

"Frank Vega's wife. They had an incident at their house. She's running a little scared."

"Arlo Baines. A bodyguard and a screenwriter." Ross shook his head. "Ain't that a kick in the nuts."

Thunder boomed nearby.

He lifted the tape, motioned for me to enter. I did so and followed him around the side of the building to an open metal door.

"Are we OK to enter?" I asked.

Protecting a crime scene from contamination was the primary concern of the lead investigator. Only the most essential people were allowed on-site until everything was processed.

"Techs are finished. Coroner's been and gone." He handed me a pair of white cloth booties and latex gloves. "I need you for a preliminary ID. Only one of them had a wallet."

"One of who? What are you talking about?"

Ross wobbled a little as he put on his booties, looking frail and old all of a sudden.

"Sorry, I forgot to tell you. Didn't get much sleep last night. This is a multiple, a four-top."

I hoped my face didn't reflect my shock. This was a new wrinkle, the increased bloodshed.

"I'd get one of the guys from the bus in here," he said, "but most of them don't speak English, and I'd rather have somebody I know tramping around the scene."

I tugged on the protective gear.

When we were both suited up, he stepped inside and led me down a narrow hallway.

A room lay at the end of the corridor. As we approached, I could see a number of crime scene investigators standing around, one scribbling notes on a clipboard.

I stepped into what at one time had been a storage area. Now it was outfitted as a greenroom, a sofa and several easy chairs, a bank of mirrors illuminated by makeup lights, a small kitchen area along one wall.

Ross pointed to a heavyset man on the floor next to a coffee table, one leg bent at the knee, arms outstretched above his head. The top of the purple tracksuit he wore had ridden up his body, displaying a hairy stomach.

"This is the one who had a cell phone in his hand with your email on it."

Dried blood spilled out across his face from where the bullet had entered his skull at the juncture where his eye met his nose.

"Email address says the guy's name is Pecky Ruibal." He paused. "So is this him?"

"I only saw pictures on the internet."

Ross yawned but didn't reply.

"Looks like him, though." I recognized the tracksuit and mustache.

On the sofa were two other men wearing similar clothes, both sprawled out like they were taking a nap. The one on the left had been shot in the throat, the guy on the right in the chest.

"Then I'm gonna say these guys are the other two kings, then," Ross said.

"Who's the fourth?" I pointed to a man wearing Wranglers and a western-style black shirt. He'd fallen facedown in the kitchen area, the back half of his skull missing. Blood and brain matter coated the cabinets by the refrigerator.

"He's the one with a wallet. Assistant manager at the club. Apparently, the band had a gig here tonight."

Like every other murder scene I'd ever visited, I was struck by the stillness, the dull silence of it all. Lifeless bodies positioned unnaturally, pale skin waxy and slack, drably lit by the fluorescent lights overhead. A vast emptiness permeated the room, along with the smell of blood, stale cigarette smoke, and urine.

"Collateral damage," I said.

Pecky Ruibal had been a courier, a moneyman, if I had to guess.

The drug business was a two-way endeavor—product goes one direction, cash the other. What better person than a traveling musician, one with a large tour bus, to run currency back to the border?

Ross cocked his head. "What are you talking about?"

A wave of melancholy engulfed me.

He frowned like he was trying to figure out something.

"Fito Alvarez," I said. "The guy I told you about two days ago. You need to get eyes on him."

"How come?" Ross asked. "Because your drunk boss doesn't like the way he dresses?"

I wanted to say because he was investigating these murders, too, while working for both the cartel and the feds. But that was too much to go into right now.

"You think Fito did this?" he asked.

I shook my head. "No. But I think he can give you more than I can."

Ross snorted. "What the hell does that mean?"

I didn't answer.

"So I gotta ask you about this." He held up a plastic evidence bag containing a smartphone. "Tell me about the email, Mr. Screenwriter."

I looked around the room for a video camera. There wasn't one.

"It's like you wanted to talk to him," Ross said, "but you didn't want to say about what."

A walkie-talkie on his belt chirped, followed by a voice saying the ambulances were on their way and what should we do about the reporters.

He turned down the volume. "Almost like you knew he might be murdered."

I did, courtesy of Throckmorton's list, which came from the DEA.

Ross tossed the bag on the coffee table. "I need you to tell me that you didn't know ahead of time this guy was gonna get bagged and tagged."

Throckmorton had been right to suggest that we just walk away. The body count was too high, and there were too many unknowns. Let the feds sort everything out. That was their job.

In another place or another time, I might have agreed with that suggestion.

But in the here and now, someone had threatened one of my tribe, the most vulnerable member, Miguel. So I was going to see this through to the end. Fito's end, if nothing else.

I took a deep breath. "Call your buddy Throckmorton."

One of the techs looked at me, eyes wide in surprise.

"Why?" Ross said. "This is Dallas PD's jurisdiction."

I didn't say anything.

"You get that you're pinging my radar as a person of interest in a multiple homicide?"

I nodded.

"Then tell me why I should talk to Throckmorton."

All three crime scene techs were looking at us, waiting to see what was coming next. If there was a leak in the Dallas Police Department, if someone was on the cartel's payroll, it wouldn't be long before they knew about me and the email I'd sent. From there, they could piece together that I had access to the list.

"Let's talk outside." I headed down the hallway to the exit door. Ross followed.

The sky was blacker still, the wind stronger. A news van was parked on the street, and a camera crew stood in front of the tour bus.

Four dead bodies meant this was going to be a major story, not just a couple of lines in the metro section of the paper. It wouldn't take long for someone to connect the crime today to Sandoval and the man who owned the restaurant.

Questions would be asked. What was the common thread among the victims? How could the Dallas police let this happen? Was there a serial killer on the loose?

I pulled off the booties and gloves.

"I checked out Fito," Ross said. "He's a cop on loan to the feds. Why're you trying to jam him up?"

"They're not the only people he's working for," I said.

He frowned. "What the hell are you saying?"

"What do you think I'm saying?"

A moment passed.

Ross swore as the rain began to fall.

- CHAPTER TWENTY-FOUR -

I jogged back to my truck, hoping to get inside before the rain started in earnest.

I'd just reached the driver's side when a gray Ford Expedition screeched to a stop a few yards in front of me.

All the doors popped open at the same time.

Four men wearing blue windbreakers exited.

They split up. Two approached Ross. One stayed by their vehicle.

The fourth strode in my direction. He was in his late thirties with a buzz haircut and a thick mustache. He glanced at Quinn in the passenger seat and then turned to me.

"You Arlo Baines?"

"Maybe. Who are you?" I tried not to let it show how unhappy I was that he knew my name.

"Special Agent Flynn. Drug Enforcement Administration."

I looked at the two men talking to Ross, saw the DEA markings on the back of their windbreakers. Ross didn't appear to be very happy. He was pointing to the club and the tour bus, an angry expression on his face.

"I've heard about you," Agent Flynn said. "Everybody says you're a stand-up guy." He mentioned a couple of officers I'd work with at the Rangers. "Too bad you're not still on the job. We need men like you."

I wasn't a big fan of people blowing smoke up my ass, so I didn't say anything.

"We understand you've been looking into a series of murders—unofficially, of course."

"Old habits are hard to kick," I said. "You know how it is."

"I hear you, brother." He smiled. "But this is a situation you shouldn't get involved in. Sleeping dogs and all."

We were both silent for a few seconds, sizing each other up.

I nodded because that seemed like what he wanted. "Message received."

He nodded back, satisfied.

"One question," I said. "Do you know where I can find Fito Alvarez? I need to talk to him."

Special Agent Flynn grimaced like he had indigestion. "That would be part of the sleeping-dogs thing I just mentioned. Not asking questions about him."

"You realize he's working for a drug cartel in addition to you guys, right?"

Flynn rolled his eyes, a flash of anger crossing his face. "Boy, you are a self-righteous asshole, aren't you? You ever even been to South Texas?"

I didn't answer, wary after his sudden shift in mood.

"Different world down there. Like its own separate country."

I glanced at Quinn, remembered her stories about the videos. A bolt of lightning ripped across the sky, followed immediately by thunder.

"Half of Alvarez's family lives in Acuña," Flynn said. "Right in the thick of it. He's got a lot of balls in the air."

I tried to look like I gave a damn about Fito Alvarez and his airborne balls. He was a dirty cop. Whatever his situation was didn't give him the right to threaten someone close to me.

"So what's the story inside?" I pointed to the club, hoping a small part of him still regarded me as a brother officer.

He didn't reply. He just gave me a blank stare that managed to convey apathy as to whether I lived or died as well as hostility, all in one look.

"Tell me and I'll go away. I promise."

Flynn's blank look was replaced with an expression of smugness.

"Just talked to the cops who interviewed the people on the bus," he said. "Whoever the shooter is, he messed up this time. They'll have an arrest in a day or so."

I arched an eyebrow but didn't speak, counting on his need to brag.

"They ID'd the shooter's car," he said. "A Honda Prelude, black, tinted windows."

• • •

The rain started as soon as I got in the pickup. A few drops followed by a deluge.

Quinn asked what happened. I told her about the four murdered men inside the club and the conversation with the DEA agent, how they knew what kind of car the killer drove.

The words spilled out of their own accord, my brain worrying over the Honda that Miguel was so fond of and the vehicle's connection to Javier's acquaintance.

Could Gusano be the killer? It wouldn't be the first time a cartel had subcontracted out a piece of work, in this case hiring La Eme to take out the Vaqueros' people. Something about that scenario didn't feel right, however.

The rain fell in sheets, pinging the skin of my truck like pebbles on a tin roof.

Quinn asked if I had any idea where Fito was, how he might react. I had no answers or even reasonable guesses.

Outside, the storm raged, federal agents and police officers scurrying about, trying not to be swept away.

I cranked the ignition.

"Where are we going?" she asked.

"To find a Honda Prelude."

• • •

My pickup splashed through a puddle in the parking lot of the Players Inn, across the street from Mendoza's Auto Salvage.

I stepped on the brakes, and the truck skidded to a stop.

The sky was overcast, but the rain had tapered off, leaving the city wet, hot, and gray.

Only a few hours had passed since I'd been here, but it seemed like weeks.

"Is something on fire?" Quinn pointed to a puff of smoke that looked like it was coming from the rear of the property.

"The warehouse with the cars." I swore, pressed the gas.

The pickup jumped across Davis Street, entering the salvage yard going way too fast.

Quinn braced an arm on the dash as my truck careened toward the rear of the property, zigzagging through piles of rusted metal parts and junked autos.

The roll-up door on the warehouse was open. Inside, flames had engulfed the Honda.

I stopped the pickup about sixty feet away, watching the best lead we had be destroyed. A moment later, the gas tank on the Honda blew, spewing flames on the other two vehicles.

"Cameras," I said.

A chop shop and an auto salvage yard, Gusano had to have video on this place.

"I need to check the office for video." I slammed the transmission into reverse and turned the truck around. I headed toward the office on the other side of the property, driving just as fast as before, Quinn bouncing in her seat.

We had to move quickly, before anybody showed up because of the fire. I parked by the front door.

A Harley sat to one side of the entrance, the only mode of transport visible other than the junked autos.

Despite the presence of the motorcycle, the place felt empty. A fire raged at the rear of the property, so you'd think Gusano or whoever would be outside, seeing what was going on.

"Wait here." I grabbed a pair of latex gloves from the floorboard.

Quinn glanced around the salvage yard, the metal hulks, the corroding auto parts. "Not a chance."

"Stay out of the way, then." I got out and strode to the front of the office.

She followed me to the door.

I motioned for her to stand to one side, out of the line of fire. I tugged on the gloves, positioned myself on the opposite side, and pressed on the door.

It swung open. Unlatched.

Quinn looked at me with wide eyes.

I pulled the Glock from my waistband and waited, silently counting to ten, then stepped inside.

The office for Mendoza's Auto Salvage was small, maybe thirty by thirty, paneled in wood, the vinyl-tiled floor scarred from years of dirty shoes.

A desk sat in the middle of the room, covered with papers and files. A calendar hung on one wall, a bikini-clad model lounging on a stack of tires.

Two doors were at the rear of the office. One was marked with a RESTROOM sign.

The other was partially open, leading to what looked like a storeroom, a likely spot for the video system to be located.

I walked around the desk, past a transmission and several car batteries, and stopped at the doorway leading to the storeroom.

Quinn moved to my side. She swore quietly at the same time that I saw the legs on the floor, just visible inside the entrance.

Dirty coveralls, grimy sneakers. Not moving.

I pushed open the door, stepped into a small room with a copier by one wall, shelves on the other.

Gusano lay on his back, lifeless eyes open, staring at the ceiling. He'd been shot twice in the chest.

"What is happening?" Quinn's voice was tinged with panic.

"The killer's tying up loose ends." I knelt by the body, felt for a pulse on one wrist.

Nothing but the warmth of his skin. Gusano had been dead only a few minutes.

A card table sat by the copier, a small computer with a twelve-inch monitor on top. Wires and coax cables ran from the back of the computer to a hole in the rear wall of the storeroom.

The computer was really a DVR, one big hard drive, storage for the video surveillance system, similar to what we had at the Aztec Bazaar. The view from every camera recorded automatically, the footage deleting itself after a period of time, usually three or four weeks.

The device was dark gray, so the bullet holes were hard to see until you got up close.

Three of them in a row, diagonally across the top, destroying the hard drive inside.

Quinn pointed to the ruined DVR. "Is that what you're looking for?"

I nodded.

"Whoever he is, he's thorough," she said.

I was about to reply when I heard the sound of footsteps on the vinyl-tiled floor.

The obese ponytailed guy from this morning stood in the doorway of the storeroom.

He looked at Gusano's body and then at me. "What the hell is going on?"

- CHAPTER TWENTY-FIVE -

No one spoke for a few seconds.

The ponytailed guy blinked several times like he couldn't believe what he was seeing, his buddy dead on the floor.

"Somebody killed Gusano," I said.

He looked at the Glock in my hand, took a step back.

I put the gun in my waistband. "I think we just missed the killer."

He pointed to the body. "You know who that is? You got any idea?"

"We didn't do this," Quinn said. "You have to believe us."

He looked at her like he was seeing her for the first time. He took several more steps back until he hit the desk.

I walked out of the storeroom. Quinn followed.

"Do you know about the cars in the second warehouse?" I asked.

He didn't speak, just kept looking back and forth between the two of us, eyes wide.

"Gusano was letting somebody use a Honda Prelude," I said. "We need to know who."

"Do you know what the bounty's gonna be?" he asked.

"What are you talking about?" I realized the front door was open, and one or more people were just outside.

"On you," he said. "Because you took out Gusano. He's a freaking captain."

He had to be referring to La Eme.

Gusano must have been a higher-up in the organization. He was now dead, and I'd been seen standing over the still-warm body, holding a gun.

I shook my head. "I didn't kill him."

Ponytail flexed his fingers, telegraphing his intent.

I reached for the Glock right as he charged.

His head hit my sternum, a hippo stomping on my chest.

I fell backward, dropped the gun.

He landed on top of me, which was bad and good.

Bad because he weighed as much as an entire village in Ethiopia. Good in that he couldn't do much damage with his arms and legs.

After a couple of seconds, he rolled off, tried to stand, a tough task when you weighed that much.

Still on the ground, I struggled to fill my lungs with air, then elbowed his face, aiming for the nose but ending up striking his lips.

From the front of the office, I heard footsteps, exclamations in Spanish.

One problem at a time.

Ponytail lay on his side, one hand held to his mouth, trying to hit me with the other.

I kneed him in the stomach, my knee disappearing into a foot or so of blubber.

He stopped trying to hit me.

I slammed the fleshy part of my palm into his nose.

Quinn screamed.

I scrambled to my feet, wobbly, chest aching, hoping Ponytail was out of the game for the next few seconds at least.

A Hispanic man wearing an oversize white T-shirt and a heavy gold chain around his neck stood in the doorway. He held a pistol sideways like he was in a bad action movie from the nineties.

He aimed at Quinn, who was across the room, clutching my Glock.

He fired. And missed.

She screamed again, yanked the trigger. She didn't miss.

The thug in the doorway made a sound between a burp and a hiccup. A bright-red spot about the size of a marble appeared in the middle of his chest.

The spot grew larger, staining the white T-shirt.

He dropped his gun, fell to the floor.

I dashed to the doorway, carefully peered outside.

A Cadillac Escalade was parked by my pickup, both front doors open. It appeared to be empty, and no one else was around.

I turned to face the office.

Quinn was staring at the dead thug on the floor, one hand against her mouth, the other still holding my Glock.

"Give me the gun," I said.

She didn't react, breathing shallow, pistol still up, her finger on the trigger.

I approached her from the side, avoiding the muzzle, and slid my hand around hers, trying to ease the weapon from her grasp.

Grunting from across the room.

Ponytail was standing. Blood streamed down his chest from the damage to his nose and mouth.

He held a gun in his hand the correct way, where the odds of missing were greatly lessened. He brought the weapon up, aiming at me.

Only milliseconds before he pulled the trigger.

No time to take the Glock from Quinn's hand.

I slid my index finger on top of hers, jerked the pistol toward Ponytail. Pressed the trigger.

Quinn yelped as the pistol bucked in her hand.

The bullet hit Ponytail in the cheekbone.

His head snapped back. He dropped the weapon. Landed on the floor with a *thud* that shook the foundation.

Quinn fell against me.

I braced her with my free arm, taking the Glock from her hand with the other.

She turned in to me, burying her head in the space between my neck and shoulder.

I held her for a moment before pushing her away.

"We need to leave," I said.

She placed a hand on the desk, palm on top of a tool catalog, trying to steady herself.

I grabbed the two pistols on the floor, Ponytail's and the guy in the white T-shirt's.

"Are they dead?" she asked. "B-b-both of them?"

I nodded, making a mental list of all the possible ways this could come back on us. Too many to count. At least I'd been wearing gloves.

"Did you touch anything?" I asked.

"Just the g-gun." She moved her hand from the desk.

I decided not to mention the catalog. She was shaky enough already. There was a small paper sack on the floor. I grabbed the sack and placed the three pistols inside, followed by the catalog with her palm print.

"Let's get out of here." I tucked the sack under my arm.

- CHAPTER TWENTY-SIX -

I drove down Davis Street, heading toward the highway, careful to stay under the speed limit. In the rearview mirror, I could see a column of oily smoke snaking skyward.

It was late Saturday afternoon, and there was very little traffic in this part of town. Nobody was parked in front of the Players Inn, no police or firefighters rushing to the scene yet.

Quinn sat in the passenger seat, shaking uncontrollably, the paper sack with the guns in her lap.

I turned onto Loop 12 and headed north, away from Mendoza's and the three dead thugs, away from the Aztec Bazaar and Javier. Away from Miguel.

When we reached Interstate 30, I headed west toward Fort Worth.

"Wh-where are w-w-we going?" Quinn's teeth chattered as she spoke.

"We need to get you something to eat."

"I'm not hungry."

"Food'll calm you down."

Eating would keep her hands busy, engage her brain, the rote activity soothing. Plus, the bustle in a restaurant would give her something to think about beyond the fact that she had just smoked a member of the Mexican Mafia.

An IHOP lay about a mile away, and that was my ultimate destination. Before that, however, we had a stop to make.

The Elm Fork of the Trinity River cut through this section of town. There were very few buildings. Lots of vacant land, heavily wooded.

I exited at MacArthur, drove north until we reached a narrow dirt road just before a bridge that crossed the river.

The road led to a spot under the bridge where people sometimes fished, trying their hand at whatever the muddy waters had to offer, usually channel cats and alligator gar.

I slowed and turned onto the dirt path. A few yards later, I parked under the bridge and exited the pickup, taking a moment to check out the surroundings. No fishermen were present. No sounds but the traffic on the bridge above. The air smelled like water and damp soil.

I walked to Quinn's side. Knocked on the glass.

She rolled down the window.

"Give me the sack," I said.

She frowned, still shaking.

"We need to lose the guns." I pointed to the river.

"B-b-but we have to have a weapon."

"No, we don't." I shook my head.

I could have wiped down everything and removed her prints, but the last thing we needed right now was to be in possession of any firearms connected to a homicide.

"Are you sure?" she asked. "What if they come back?"

"We'll be OK. I promise."

After a moment, she gave me the paper sack.

I walked to the edge of the river, about ten feet away. There, I tossed the bag into the middle of the water and watched it sink.

I would have preferred to find a power drill and bore out the barrel of my Glock, rendering a ballistics match impossible. But that meant stopping at a hardware store, a place with cameras and witnesses. The faster the evidence disappeared, the better.

I got back in the truck.

Quinn hugged herself, still shivering.

"Let's get you something to eat," I said.

• • •

We sat in a corner booth at the rear of the IHOP.

The place was nearly empty. A handful of people in the front, truck driver types, and a Dallas County constable at the counter.

Even though it was late in the afternoon, I ordered breakfast food for both of us.

Bacon and eggs, pancakes and hash browns. A pot of coffee.

When the waitress left, I said, "How are you feeling?"

"How am I supposed to feel?" Quinn glanced at the constable.

Numb, shaky. Remorseful, maybe angry. Fearful. Certainly jittery.

I decided not to mention any of that. Also, the sleep issues and nightmares that were to come.

"Should we call the police?" she asked.

I didn't answer, hoping she could figure out the danger of that particular action on her own.

"What choice did I have?" She crossed her arms. "That guy was going to kill you . . . me . . . us."

"You did what needed to be done."

Across the room, the constable paid his bill, headed for the exit.

When the door shut behind him, Quinn said, "I need to tell Frank."

"I wouldn't if I were you."

She frowned. "You don't trust my husband?"

"That's not the issue."

"What, then?"

I took a moment, pondering the best way to say what she needed to hear. "The smartest thing you can do is to never ever talk about what happened today. Not to anybody."

"But I killed a man."

"And you'll have to live with that the rest of your life." I paused. "But the more people who know, the higher the odds are that you'll end up in prison. Or worse."

The waitress brought our food, refilled our water glasses, asked if we needed anything else. When she left, Quinn pushed away her plate. I pushed it back, told her to eat.

She took a couple of hesitant bites and then dug in like she hadn't taken nourishment in a week. We ate in silence for a few minutes.

"What's going to happen?" she asked. "Back there at the salvage yard."

"The police'll run the ballistics on the bullets that killed the three men. My Glock is clean, so the bullets in the two hoods we shot won't ping anywhere."

She put down her fork.

"But Gusano's gonna be a different story," I said. "I'm willing to bet the round that killed him came from the same gun that killed Sandoval, Pecky Ruibal, and the restaurant guy."

She took a sip of coffee, stared out the window.

I continued. "That, combined with the other two dead thugs and the massacre at the club, is gonna make heads spin with the Dallas police."

"The media," she said. "They'll have a field day with this."

Along with the DEA, the competing cartel, and the powers that be at La Eme. I didn't say anything.

The waitress took our plates, refilled our cups. We sat without talking for a while, drinking coffee.

"You ever fired a gun before?" I asked.

She nodded. "Frank taught me. He has a lot of guns. He's a pretty good shot."

There was an interesting tidbit.

She'd brought her overnight bag in with her, not wanting to leave it in the truck, the post-violence paranoia setting in, the need to guard, to protect. She picked up the bag from the floor, ready to leave.

"Frank's not a killer," she said. "If that's what you're thinking."

"What is he, then?"

Her brow furrowed. "An angry man. But not a killer."

I didn't reply because there was no sense contradicting her.

One thing I'd learned as a cop. Anyone could commit murder.

- CHAPTER TWENTY-SEVEN -

Despite the assurances I'd given Quinn earlier, I knew we needed a weapon.

I'd spent most of my adult life with a pistol on my hip. Ditching the compromised Glock left me feeling exposed, underdressed, like I had on summer beachwear at a black-tie ball.

Back in the pickup, I asked Quinn how she was doing. She said fine, the eating helped, thanks for insisting. I told her she was going to feel wired for the next few days, senses heightened, emotional for no reason, that sort of thing. She shrugged, eyes half-closed, food coma setting in.

I pulled out of the IHOP parking lot and headed back to town, avoiding the area around Mendoza's, since it was likely to be crawling with police.

My destination was a gun shop on Irving Boulevard, a small place sandwiched between a print shop and a nude-modeling studio.

In addition to dealing in firearms, the owner was an occasional loan shark and seller of stolen jewelry, the latter being how I'd met him back when I was a law enforcement officer.

He'd tried to sell a diamond pendant to the husband of the woman who'd had the item stolen in the first place. Words were exchanged, threats made, and at least one shot fired before I'd arrived on the scene. The husband was reluctant to press charges because of a heretofore undisclosed relationship with one of the nude models, so no arrest was made.

I parked by the front door.

The proprietor owned the entire building as well as the modeling studio and lived in the back, in a section that jutted behind the print shop.

Quinn and I exited, meeting at the front of the store.

A sign on the metal door read **Stodghill's Fine Sporting Goods— Please call for an appointment.** I rang the bell and looked up at the camera mounted under the eaves.

An intercom attached to one side of the door crackled to life, and a disembodied voice said, "What part of 'call first' don't you understand, Arlo?"

"Are you closed?" I asked.

"I'm always closed."

"I need a gun. Sooner rather than later."

A moment of silence followed by the buzz of a solenoid releasing a dead bolt.

I pushed open the door, stepped into a room that was long and narrow. A glass display counter ran along one wall. The display was filled with handguns along with various knives and expensive-looking flashlights. The gun racks on the wall behind the counter were filled as well—a few hunting weapons and lots of assault rifles.

A heavy wooden door on the back wall opened, and Stodghill entered the room. He wore a multipocket khaki vest over a white oxford cloth shirt, concealment for who knew how many guns on his person, and an LBJ-style Stetson.

"Look what the bobcat dragged in." He ambled to a spot behind the counter, plopped his hands on the glass. After a moment, his attention focused on Quinn.

"Something from the LadySmith & Wesson line, perhaps?"

She shook her head. "I don't like guns."

Stodghill's eyes narrowed. He squinted at her like he was trying to figure something out.

Quinn didn't make eye contact with him.

After a moment, Stodghill turned to me, one eyebrow raised. "You mentioned needing a firearm?"

I told him what I wanted.

"What happened to the one I sold you a couple of months ago?"

"I need another one. You keeping score or what?"

He opened his mouth like he was going to reply. Then he looked at Quinn again.

"Forgive the intrusion, but is everything all right?"

"Yes, of course," she said. "Why wouldn't it be?"

He stared at her for a moment and then blinked several times, breaking his trance, and turned toward me.

"Let me get one from the back." He disappeared into the rear.

Quinn started shaking again. She looked at me, eyes fearful.

I stepped closer, grasped her arm, afraid she might faint.

"I don't feel so good," she said.

"Take deep breaths. In and out."

She did as I told her, leaning against me, steadying herself. After a moment, her coloring improved.

"Why don't you wait in the truck?" I pointed to the door.

She nodded and left.

A minute later, Stodghill returned carrying a box and a clipboard. "Where'd your friend go?"

"Getting some fresh air." I handed over my driver's license for the background check.

Stodghill held the license in his hand and stared at the front door. Then he started the paperwork.

Ten minutes later, I stuck the new pistol in the spot behind my hip.

"Thanks for the gun." I headed to the exit. After a few feet, I stopped, turned back around. "You got a silencer for this?"

He cocked his head but didn't reply.

"You do sell them, right?"

"I can get 'em," he said. "If you have the right paperwork."

A silencer was the equivalent of a machine gun in the eyes of the law. Legal to own if you paid an exorbitant federal tax and navigated your way through a jungle of red tape. You couldn't just plop down your money and a few minutes later walk out the door with one.

Silencers and machine guns were available illegally, but not as readily as one might think, the prison sentences for trafficking or possessing either item without the proper paperwork being stiff and mandatory.

"You sold any lately?" I asked.

He stared at me without replying, eyes deadpan.

"You been reading the papers? Heard about the murders by the bazaar?"

"Where you going with this, Arlo?"

I didn't answer.

"There's a cone of silence here at the gun store," he said. "I don't kiss and tell."

"Fair enough."

"You need anything else?"

I shook my head.

"Next time, call first." He paused. "Or better yet, go somewhere else."

• • •

Quinn was already in the truck.

I hopped in behind the wheel, cranked the ignition.

"He knew, didn't he?" She stared at the front of the shop.

"Knew what?"

"The way he looked at me. He could tell something bad had happened."

"He doesn't know anything, and he never will, so long as neither of us talks about what went down at Mendoza's." I turned on the AC.

"I've met him before," she said. "A long time ago. He'll remember eventually."

I was about to put the transmission into gear. I stopped, my hand on the lever.

"Frank did some legal work for him." She paused. "What if he says something to Frank?"

"What would he say? I saw your wife, and she looked nervous?"

She didn't reply.

I felt my phone vibrate. I looked at the screen, read the message from Kiki. I yanked the transmission into gear.

"What's wrong?" Quinn asked.

"Miguel is missing."

- CHAPTER TWENTY-EIGHT -

They'd had a good time at the zoo, Kiki told me.

They saw the apes and the giraffes, a crocodile and a rhinoceros. And the zebras, oh how Miguel loved the zebras.

After the zoo, they'd come home. Kiki's son, the one closest in age to Miguel, had gotten sick, a stomach thing; you know how kids are.

They were going to order pizza instead of going to Chuck E. Cheese's. Kiki had put her son to bed while the rest of her brood, along with Miguel and several kids from the neighborhood, had gone outside to resurrect the soccer game from the day before.

Her husband, Tony, ordered the pizza and then popped a beer, relaxing in front of the TV, the children visible in the backyard through the window.

Everything was fine until the rain started.

Then the kids trooped inside, muddy and wet, jabbering with each other.

There were so many of them, she said. So many it was hard to keep track. And the lightning and the thunder, the noise from the video games. The general chaos.

That was why it took a while to notice Miguel wasn't there.

Quinn and I were in Kiki's living room. She stood beside her husband, eyes filled with tears. The children were in another part of the house.

"I'm sorry, Arlo. I don't know how this could have happened." She wiped her eyes. "Have you checked his cell?"

I'd bought Miguel a phone several weeks before, a safety measure, a way to keep track of his location.

The problem was, unlike every other kid on the planet, he didn't like carrying the device. Javier speculated that his reluctance must have had something to do with the people he'd been with after his parents had died, who I now knew to be a gang affiliated with one of the cartels.

"I looked already," I said. "His cell is off."

The last location was Kiki's house, so at least he'd had the phone with him. I wondered if he had turned it off or if someone else had done so.

The rain had stopped. Early evening sunlight filtered through the room. The TV was on mute; toys littered the floor.

"You want me to call the police?" Tony asked.

And tell them what? I wanted to say. A boy with no parents or legal guardians, one who didn't even exist in the eyes of the law, was missing?

I shook my head. "Let's start at the beginning. Describe for me everything you saw when you got home."

Kiki and Tony stared at me blankly.

"You turned onto your street," I said. "And then what? Did you see any cars or people who didn't belong? A repair truck, a UPS guy, anything?"

They thought about it for a moment, glancing at each other. Finally, Tony shook his head.

"Did you notice anybody following you on the way home from the zoo?" I asked.

"I don't think so." Kiki looked at her husband. "Did we?"

Tony shook his head again.

"What about at the zoo itself?" I asked. "Anything unusual happen?"

"No," Kiki said. "Everything was fine. We all had a good time."

"What do the other children say?" Quinn spoke for the first time.

Kiki crossed her arms, obviously uncomfortable with having the well-to-do Quinn Vega in her modest home.

"Nothing," Tony said. "One minute he was there, and then he wasn't."

"I'm going to want to talk to them," I said.

"Of course." Kiki left the room.

Thirty minutes later, I'd visited with all the children, even Kiki's son with the stomach bug.

Nobody remembered anything.

They'd been playing soccer, but Miguel hadn't wanted to participate. It took some artful questions, but gradually I picked up on the fact that the children regarded Miguel as odd. He wanted to be part of their activities, but he was reserved, like something was holding him back.

If you're forced to work as a prepubescent assassin, I guess that makes you a little off.

I turned to Tony and said, "Let me see the backyard."

He led Quinn and me outside.

Even at this time of day, the air was hot, the humidity thick because of the storm.

We marched across the wet grass to a wooden gate leading to the alley.

"This is the only way out," Tony said. "I keep it locked on this side with a—"

He stopped talking when it became apparent the gate was no longer secure.

I pointed to a carabiner lying on the grass. "Is that what you use to keep the gate locked?"

He nodded, looking perplexed. "I don't understand. There's no way into the yard except through the house."

"He left of his own accord. He wasn't kidnapped." Quinn looked at me. "That's good, right? No one's taken him."

I remembered the dread I felt when I'd heard about my family's death. Icy sweat all over my body, brain not functioning right. Right now, in Kiki's backyard, the air felt cold. My vision tunneled, sounds muffled.

My mind raced, trying to figure out where a street kid from the border region of Mexico would go in Dallas, an unfamiliar city.

More important, I tried to figure out why he would leave Kiki's home, a place where he felt safe.

What could make him leave?

After a moment, I realized *what* wasn't the right question.

Who could make him leave?

- CHAPTER TWENTY-NINE -

We searched the neighborhood, Quinn and I in my pickup, Tony in his vehicle. Kiki stayed at the house with the other children.

We drove in ever expanding circles, checking out alleys and side streets, vacant lots and half-built homes, the hiding places of the neighborhood.

Nothing.

After an hour, we returned to Kiki's house.

Eight in the evening. The sun was setting, but it was still hot. Quinn stayed in the truck, kept the air-conditioning on.

Kiki met me in the front yard. "I'm so sorry, Arlo."

"It's not your fault." I tried to smile. Tried to show my sincerity, to indicate that I wasn't placing any blame on her.

But my facial muscles wouldn't respond. My cheeks felt wooden and numb. Fear coiled itself around my gut, my palms clammy.

"We'll put the kids to bed," Tony said. "Then I'll go out again."

"Thank you."

"Have you told Javier?" Kiki asked.

I shook my head.

"I'm so sorry." She leaned against her husband.

This time I didn't know if she was sorry about Miguel or that I would have to tell her boss. I got back in the pickup, dreading what would come next.

Quinn said, "Are you OK?"

I put the transmission into drive. "I have to talk to Javier."

• • •

El Corazón Roto was rocking, Saturday night in full swing.

People stood three deep at the bar, customers occupying every seat. From the back corner, the jukebox blared accordion music.

Even with the AC, the room felt warm, the air heavy with the smell of sweat and alcohol.

Several men cast appraising glances at Quinn Vega when we entered, staring at her trim figure in the skinny jeans and form-fitting, sleeveless blouse. There weren't very many women in the place, a half dozen at most, and she was the only one who looked like she didn't work on a lube rack.

The bartender caught my eye. He jerked his thumb toward the rear.

The crowd grew thicker as we made our way toward the back. Quinn grasped my hand as I threaded my way through the people. Her touch felt warm and comforting, a soothing moment in an otherwise desperate time.

Javier was alone, sitting in the same booth that Aloysius Throckmorton had used two days before. A bottle of Modelo and an empty shot glass sat in front of him.

He looked up. "Well, what do we have here?"

Quinn let go of my hand.

"I need to talk to you," I said.

"Have a drink first." He enunciated each word carefully, the way people do when they're intoxicated but don't want others to know.

I shook my head.

"You too good to drink with a Mexican?" he asked.

I laughed in spite of the circumstances. "All the time I've been working here, you think I don't like Mexicans?"

He stared across the room but didn't reply.

"How about I get us some coffee?" Quinn asked.

"Get whatever the hell you want," Javier said. "Just tell the bartender I'm ready for another round."

She glanced at me, wordlessly asking what to do next. I pointed to an empty spot at the end of the bar, told her to wait there. She snaked her way through the crowd and hopped onto a barstool that had just freed up.

A new tune started playing on the jukebox, one of the so-called *narcocorridos*, a song glorifying the cartels, Robin Hoods of the modern era in the eyes of certain people.

The song served as a reminder that for all the death and devastation visited upon society by organizations like the Vaqueros, there were some who held them in high regard. The cartels offered an opportunity for the little man to succeed, a chance for greatness. They also promised adventure, the romance of battle, something men had dreamed about since the invention of spears and fermented beverages.

"We need to talk." I sat across from Javier.

"You find out who killed Sandoval?"

I tried to breathe through my mouth, the stench of alcohol coming off him overpowering.

"What kind of investigator are you?" he asked, one eyelid drooping.

"How much have you had to drink?"

"*Besa mi culo, puta.* That's how much."

Translation: *kiss my ass, bitch.* Subtext: he'd had *a lot* to drink. And he was angry. Booze and rage, never a good combination.

The anger served as a mask for the sadness, a coping mechanism I was all too familiar with. I felt the weight of his loss mix with mine, a sodden overcoat settling on my shoulders, pulling me down.

"There's something I need to tell you," I said.

He whistled at the bartender, the sound shrill and loud even in the crowded bar. He held up the empty bottle and shot glass.

"Javier." I leaned close. "Miguel is missing."

No reply.

"He left Kiki's. Didn't tell anybody anything."

The bartender brought over another round and left.

Javier took a drink from the fresh beer.

"Did you hear me?" I said.

He nodded but didn't speak, his face blank. A moment passed.

"Did you take him?" I asked.

The thought had crossed my mind as we drove away from Kiki's. Miguel was pretty levelheaded, all things considered. He wouldn't have just left without good reason.

"He doesn't belong with you," Javier said.

"What the hell are you talking about?" I felt a red-hot rage shoot down my arms and legs. "Because I'm white? Is that it?"

No reply.

"He wasn't with me," I said. "He was with Kiki. And her kids. They all went to the zoo, like a normal family."

Javier downed his shot.

"You know how worried we all were?" I asked.

He shrugged.

"If you and I weren't friends," I said, "I'd take you outside and—"

He cut me off, face reddening, his anger matching mine. "I wanted to see the boy. You can't keep him from me."

I closed my eyes for a moment, tried to remain calm. "You could have just called. Nobody's trying to keep anything from you."

He looked over at Quinn. "Are you fucking the landlord's wife now?"

"That's me, the man slut. Don't change the subject." I took a deep breath. "Where is Miguel?"

"Have a drink with me, Arlo. Let's don't fight." He smiled, trying to be friendly.

His irrationality was maddening. Booze-induced mood swings, grief, anger, everything competing.

"I don't want a damn drink. I want to see Miguel."

Javier took a long pull of beer. "He's with Maria."

I realized then he didn't think of the boy as I did, like a youngster who needed nurturing, both physically and emotionally. In Javier's eyes, Miguel represented a way to fulfill his own needs.

A surrogate son, someone to patch the hole left by the deaths of his own children.

But not a real person. More like a puppy, something he could play with when it was convenient and then pawn off on someone else so he could wallow in grief and get shit-faced.

"We can't keep doing this," I said. "It's not fair to the boy. He needs a home."

Javier looked like he was going to say something, but he stopped when Quinn Vega materialized by the table, a terrified expression on her face.

She slid next to me in the booth, pointed toward the bar. "He's here."

I looked in the direction she indicated.

Through the crowd, I could see Fito Alvarez standing by the beer taps, smiling and laughing. He appeared relaxed, talking to a pale-skinned Latino in his thirties wearing a hunter-green polo shirt.

The man in the polo shirt turned. He had a wine-colored birthmark on his face.

Pax Larson-Ibarra. Frank Vega's client and the man I'd seen in the Sandoval backyard.

"Is there another way out?" Quinn asked.

"I'm not running from my own place," Javier said.

I pointed toward the hallway leading to the restrooms. "There's an emergency exit that way."

Quinn slid out of the booth. I stood as well, right as Fito made his way through the crowd and stopped at our table.

"Hola, amigos," he said. "How are we doing tonight?"

- CHAPTER THIRTY -

I kept my attention split between Javier and Fito.

The latter was still smiling, the picture of relaxation, not a care in the world.

Javier, on the other hand, appeared as if he was about to stroke out. He was red-faced, a vein in his temple throbbing as he clenched and unclenched his fists.

I looked at Fito. "What do you want?"

He ignored me, spoke to Quinn. "Looking good, homegirl. I like those jeans."

She crossed her arms, face pale.

"Where's your husband?" he asked. "He shouldn't let a woman like you hang out in a place like this."

"You need to leave," I said.

At the bar, Pax appeared to be buying a pitcher of beer for a man in dirty work clothes. The man smiled, shook his hand, and carried the beer to a table with two other people in similar clothes.

"I like it here," Fito said to Javier. "Good location. Not too far from the highway but off the beaten path."

Javier made a guttural sound, lips curled into a snarl.

Fito pointed to Pax on the other side of the room. "That's why me and my friend, we're gonna buy you out."

I understood immediately the attraction. From a criminal organization's point of view, acquiring the Aztec Bazaar made perfect sense.

I couldn't even begin to count the places in an operation as large as this where you could hide stuff. Executing a search warrant at a 150,000-square-foot building filled with dozens of separate businesses would take days.

Then there were the tenants themselves, many of whom paid in cash, an easy source of clean money. Those who didn't pay in cash could probably be persuaded to. Those who refused could be kicked out and replaced with businesses that were either sympathetic to the Vaqueros or owned outright by the organization.

Tire stores, maybe, like Sandoval's place. Or bus companies offering service to the border. Businesses that cashed checks and wired money internationally.

The possibilities were endless, all gathered in one central location, a social hub catering to people reluctant to talk to law enforcement.

"This operation isn't for sale," I said.

"Everything's available." Fito smiled. "The question is whether the seller knows it or not."

Javier took several deep breaths and slid from the booth. He seemed to have calmed down some. He stood up tall and straight, only wobbling a little, and looked Fito in the eye.

"You heard him," he said. "Now get out of my bar."

Fito stared at him like he was a talking dog. Amused, mildly curious at what kind of person would stand up to him.

"Even if what I have was for sale," Javier said, "I don't deal with people like you."

Fito laughed. "Look at you, being all self-righteous."

Javier staggered a little, losing his balance. He placed a hand on the back of the booth, steadied himself.

"You do business with us already, *borracho*. You bought tires from Sandoval, meals from Mariscos." Fito paused. "In this very building, you accept rent from our people."

Javier frowned. "What people?"

"Does it matter?" Fito said. "Money is money."

Cheers erupted from the front, people yelling and clapping. The bartenders pulled fresh glasses from the shelves, pouring drinks as fast as possible. Everyone's attention focused on Pax, who pulled a wad of currency from his pocket and slapped it on the bar.

"My friend," Fito said, "looks like he's buying a round for the house."

Javier sat back down, face haggard. Quinn moved to his side.

The noise in the bar grew louder as the free booze began to flow.

Fito nodded toward Javier and lowered his voice so only I could hear. "How much longer you think he's gonna last? We'll end up with this place one way or the other."

"Get out." I pointed to the door.

He moved a step closer, whispered, "Where's the car?"

I stared at him, not understanding at first.

"The Honda Prelude," he said. "We know there were witnesses who saw that vehicle when Pecky Ruibal was killed."

The murders at the club south of White Rock Lake. The guy I'd reached out to by email, the money courier.

"I don't know what you're talking about."

"Oh, I think you do. I think you've been holding out on me from the start."

The bartender brought a beer and a shot to Javier, part of Pax's gift to the bar. He glanced at me nervously and then left.

"The car leads to whoever is killing our people," Fito said. "And whoever that is, he's a dead man."

The noise grew louder still. The crowd was ecstatic with the free drinks, courtesy of everyone's new friend, Pax.

"Maybe you're the killer?" Fito arched an eyebrow.

The jukebox changed songs, another *narcocorrido*, the lyrics to this one about a man with an AK-47 and a bag of money.

"That kid you like so much is a shooter. Maybe he's your trigger man." He paused. "So, who are you working for?"

"Not the DEA, that's for sure. Unlike you."

He cocked his head, obviously surprised.

"Does Pax know about your deal with the feds?" I asked.

He chuckled. "Who do you think arranged it?"

- CHAPTER THIRTY-ONE -

Quinn helped Javier stand, then led him down the hall toward the rear exit.

Fito watched, rubbing his crotch. "She's a looker, isn't she? After all this settles down, I'm gonna have to show her what a real man is like."

"Stay away from her." I felt an overwhelming need to protect Quinn Vega.

Even as the feeling swept over me, I realized I was atoning for the past as much as anything.

Fito stared at me, eyes formed into slits like a greasy snake about to strike.

I stared back, not blinking.

"You and me are due for a little reckoning," he said.

"I'll put that on my calendar."

I'd known all along there would be consequences to challenging a man like him. His honor would demand an accounting for the perceived slights and disrespect I'd shown him.

"Back to the matter at hand," he said. "I'll bring a contract tomorrow morning, an offer for the businesses. Maybe Javier will be sober by then."

Pax was still at the bar, buying more pitchers of beer, making more friends.

Another man had joined him, the tattooed hood who'd been at the Sandovals. He had a couple of people with him, tatted up as well. The local muscle. None of them was drinking.

"If Javier doesn't accept the terms by lunch," Fito said, "sometime in the afternoon, the police will search his pickup and find a bag of cocaine."

I took a deep breath, relaxed my arms and legs, centered my concentration.

The jukebox clicked to a new song, the Texas Tornados, "Is Anybody Going to San Antone?"

"We'll make another offer the next day. The price will be half of what we're willing to pay right now."

I slumped my shoulders, feigning defeat.

Fito, sensing victory, moved closer, which was what I wanted.

"You understand what I just told you?" he asked.

I head-butted his nose, felt the satisfying crunch of cartilage against bone.

Blood jetted from his nostrils, and he fell to the ground.

The crowd was loud and boisterous. No one appeared to notice or care what had happened.

The people closest moved aside as he hit the floor, no doubt wondering what was going on.

A couple of drunks mixing it up? Well, it was Saturday night, and that was the kind of stuff that happened at a bar like El Corazón Roto.

Across the room, Pax glanced our way, a puzzled look on his face, unable to see his friend. He motioned to the tattooed hood to check out what had happened.

While the hood made his way through the crowd, I darted down the hallway leading to the rear exit.

The back door of the bar was also a side exit for the Aztec Bazaar, the two structures being attached to each other. The door opened onto a narrow corridor in the bazaar, a little-used area lined by a half dozen vacant stalls. The corridor ended about fifty feet away at a wide walkway running perpendicular to it. The walkway was one of the main thoroughfares of the bazaar.

I jogged to the intersection of the corridor and the walkway and looked in both directions.

This time of night on a Saturday, most of the stores were closed, everybody at home resting up for tomorrow, the biggest day of the week.

The only illumination came from a series of overhead fluorescents that served as emergency lighting. The walkway was dim, shadowy.

To the left, I could see two figures moving away from me—Quinn and Javier, the latter leaning on the former as they inched away from the bar.

I loped toward them.

When I was about ten feet away, Javier stumbled. Quinn tried to catch him but got tangled in his legs, and they both went down.

I helped Quinn to her feet. Javier was out cold, snoring softly.

"What happened back there?" she asked.

"I broke Fito's nose. Wasn't my smartest move, but I'd had enough of him."

"Sometimes talking is a waste of time." She pointed to Javier. "What do we do with him?"

"We need to find somewhere to lay low." I looked toward the corridor leading to the bar, hoping no one was after us yet.

She glanced that way, too. "You've disrespected Fito twice. He's not going to stop coming after you. No matter what."

"He's gonna do what he's gonna do." I grabbed Javier's arm, pulling him up and over my shoulder like a large sack of drunken potatoes. "And so am I."

Maria's shop was on the way to the front, where my truck was parked, the direction in which Quinn had been headed. I planned to continue going that way, stopping at Maria's salon for Miguel. Then I would exit the building and load everyone in my pickup so we could find somewhere to spend the night.

I lumbered toward Maria's, Javier a dead weight on my shoulder, Quinn trailing after us.

We turned the corner. This stretch of hallway was even dimmer.

I trudged on, eager to get Miguel. The journey seemed to take forever with Javier's unconscious body bouncing against my torso.

Finally, I turned the last corner. Maria's shop was ahead on the right.

They were waiting for me inside.

I stepped through the entryway and saw Fito in one of the stylist chairs, his nose swollen, blood still seeping from his nostrils. The gangbanger who'd been at the Sandovals stood next to him, holding a pistol. One of the gangbanger's friends was just inside the doorway.

I reached for my Glock, but Javier's bulk hampered my movement.

The gangbanger by the door slugged me in the stomach.

I dropped Javier and bent over, struggling for air.

The gangbanger next to Fito darted across the room and slapped the side of my head with his pistol.

I fell to the floor, and he hit me again in the same spot.

A bright white light filled my vision. Then everything went dark.

• • •

My mouth was empty, but I tasted metal.

I opened my eyes, blinked several times, saw that I was in the far corner of the shop. Javier was still passed out where I'd dropped him near the doorway.

Maria stood over me. "I told you to leave town."

Weeks before in my motel room. Her cryptic comments about how I should just keep traveling. She was part of the cartel.

"Wh-where's Miguel?" My voice was a croak.

Fito appeared next to her, a hand pressed to his nose. He pushed her aside and glared at me. "What the hell is your problem?" he asked. "All you had to do was nothing."

I felt for my Glock. Gone, as was my phone.

"You can't stop the tides," he said. "And we are the fucking ocean."

I scanned what I could see of the room. No sign of Quinn or Miguel. But then I realized there were two Fitos swimming in front of my eyes, so my vision probably couldn't be trusted 100 percent at this point.

Both Fitos aimed a gun at my face. "Who's killing our people?"

I didn't answer.

"In the end, you're gonna tell me everything you know," he said. "You won't have any secrets left. That's what they pay me for."

Despite my mouth being empty, the metal taste grew stronger. A dagger of pain shot through my skull. Now there were three Fitos.

Three Fitos and a smaller figure, shimmering and indistinct.

Miguel.

The three Fitos handed him three guns.

Miguel held the pistol like it was a piece of alien technology, like he was unsure of how to use such a bizarre device.

"The boy's with me now," Fito said. "I can use someone like him."

Miguel straightened his grip on the gun, the weapon now an extension of his arm.

Fito smiled, a teacher glad that his pupil had mastered a particularly difficult technique.

My head felt like someone had jammed a hot ice pick deep into my temple. I struggled not to vomit.

"You're going to shoot him once in the knee," Fito said to the boy. "I need some information before you kill him."

For a moment, Miguel didn't move. Then he pointed the gun at my leg.

"*Bueno.*" Fito nodded. "We'll get ice cream afterward."

Miguel's fingers grew white as his grip tightened.

Despite my messed-up vision, I stared at Miguel's face, hoping to see something—anything—that could save me. But there was nothing, just an empty void, cold and unending, a bottomless canyon.

I remembered the first time I'd laid eyes on him, months before in the bus station. Emaciated and alone, a sad little boy who needed protecting.

"It's OK, Miguel." I tried to smile. "Do what you need to do."

He took a deep breath, his arm shaking.

A long moment passed.

"Shoot him," Fito said. "Now."

Miguel closed his eyes. He turned, jammed the weapon into Fito's stomach, yanked the trigger.

The blast was loud, even muffled by the barrel being up against flesh.

Fito doubled over like a sledgehammer had hit him in the gut. He collapsed, landing on top of my legs.

A pistol was in the back of his waistband. Three of them, actually.

I reached for the middle one but came up empty-handed.

Another shot rang out.

The mirror behind me shattered.

Miguel aimed across the room at a target I couldn't see.

A woman screamed. Another blast.

Even sitting down, my balance was off, head swimming like I was drunk.

I reached once more for the gun in Fito's belt, but the taste of metal overcame me. I grasped my head to keep it from spinning.

Sounds became muted. The woman screamed again, but it seemed a long way off. Quinn or Maria, I couldn't tell. For an instant, I thought it was my wife.

I looked up as the gun in Miguel's hand bucked twice.

Empty cartridges scattered.

My eyelids felt heavy.

A few moments passed.

Miguel stood in front of me, face fearful.

I didn't remember much after that, which the doctor said was normal after a head trauma.

- CHAPTER THIRTY-TWO -

One Month Later

Gunfire woke me, the blast of a shotgun somewhere close by.

I jerked upright, disoriented. Reached for the pistol on the nightstand, the sheets falling down my torso.

Shadows splayed across the bedroom, the last of the night disappearing as dawn filtered through the windows. The dim light accentuated the drabness of the room, the faded wallpaper, scarred wooden floor, the battered dresser.

Boom.

Another shotgun blast.

I remembered where I was, the time of year.

An old farmhouse at a ranch outside of Stephenville, a small town about two hours west of Dallas. Early September, the start of hunting season for doves, all but a religious festival for certain Texans.

After a moment, my heart rate lessened. I slipped off the bed, wandered to the window.

Sunflower fields surrounded the yard, separated by barbed-wire fences. The plants represented a major food source for doves. Two men in camo T-shirts sat on hunting stools on the field side, backs to the house, shotguns resting on their laps.

The farmhouse used to be the caretaker's place, and the structure was twenty years past needing to be torn down. Aloysius Throckmorton had arranged for the lodgings as well as the old pickup in the garage, our current mode of transportation.

Miguel appeared in the doorway, a cup of coffee in one hand held out as an offering.

I padded across the room and accepted the mug.

"Did the hunters wake you?" I asked.

He didn't reply, eyes wide and empty.

"Los cazadores te despertaron?" I tried again in Spanish.

After a few seconds, he shook his head and disappeared down the hall.

He didn't talk much anymore, or sleep for that matter, not since the night he killed Fito Alvarez.

Not like he'd ever been a chatterbox, but now he was nearly mute, a few words a day at most. If circumstances were different, I'd take him to a doctor, a specialist of some kind. But doctors and hospitals meant records, a paper trail, and we'd been through too much to get caught in a trap like that.

Also, Miguel had killed an enforcer for a drug cartel, which didn't bode well for either of us.

The only medical care we had was the drunken ob-gyn who owed Throckmorton several favors and had taken care of my concussion in the aftermath of the Aztec Massacre. Unfortunately, he wasn't qualified to treat childhood emotional trauma.

That's what the media called the killings, by the way, the Aztec Massacre, despite protests by several Native American groups.

Four people had died, all by Miguel's hand.

Alphonso "Fito" Alvarez, a dirty cop from Del Rio, who might or might not have been on the DEA's payroll as an informant, depending on which alternative news website you followed.

Maria Diaz, a hairdresser supposedly in the wrong place at the wrong time.

And two street hoods with extensive criminal records, the tattooed thugs.

As of the previous night, the last time I'd checked on my burner phone, the Dallas police had no leads. The primary investigator, Detective Ross, referred reporters back to his original statement, which declared the crime to be a small-time drug deal gone bad, despite the fact that no narcotics had been found on the premises.

I took a sip of coffee and decided to pack my few belongings. Maybe it was the noise from the hunters, maybe we'd just been in one spot too long, but today felt like a good time to find a new hidey-hole.

After packing, I showered and got dressed. When I left the room, duffel over my shoulder, Miguel was in the hallway with his bag.

"Great minds think alike," I said.

He frowned, clearly not understanding the expression.

Together we cleaned up what little mess we'd made, putting everything in a plastic garbage bag that would go in the back of the truck for later disposal.

I used a rag and a bottle of glass cleaner to wipe down every surface in the house, obliterating any fingerprints we might have left.

The place was still awash with an ocean of our DNA, but our efforts would slow down any investigators, if they learned that we'd been at this location.

Outside, the sun had risen over a cloudless horizon, promising a hot day.

We waited until the hunters left their perch to retrieve a couple of downed birds. Then we jogged to the pickup, threw our stuff in the rear, and hopped in the cab.

We were gone by the time they returned to their stools, out of the yard and onto the gravel road leading to the highway. Dust trailed the old pickup as I kept the speed at a steady twenty miles per hour.

Miguel looked out the window as the sunflower fields passed by.

Hunters were everywhere, their vehicles lining the side of the road. Hopefully they were all busy searching the skies for birds, not paying attention to us.

The burner phone rang, and I answered. Only one person had the number.

"Where are you?" Throckmorton's voice on the other end.

"Driving."

"That joint from the other day," he said. "How soon can you be there?"

We'd met at a Mexican food restaurant several weeks before, when he'd given me the key and directions to the farmhouse.

"Twenty minutes."

"Toss your phone." He ended the call.

- CHAPTER THIRTY-THREE -

Lupe's Family Restaurant occupied a stucco building on a farm-to-market road a few miles outside of town.

The exterior was painted with a mural of Pancho Villa riding a longhorn bull and holding a beer stein, which made no sense to me, but I wasn't in the food service business.

The lot was about half-full, mostly pickups and work vehicles, the sun bright and hot, reflecting off the gravel. I parked underneath a hackberry tree at the edge of the lot, the nose of the truck pointing toward the highway. Throckmorton's Suburban was by the front door.

Miguel and I got out and headed inside.

The interior was decorated with piñatas and sombreros, the air smelling like grease and corn tortillas. The place was doing a good business, farmers eating breakfast, ranchers discussing the price of cattle, everybody talking about how they needed rain.

Throckmorton sat alone at a four-top in the rear of the dining area, his back to the wall.

"You lose the phone?" he asked.

I nodded and took a seat next to him, my back to the corner. I'd tossed the cell into a creek about a mile or so away.

Miguel sat across from me.

Throckmorton looked at the youngster. *"Tienes hambre?"*

No answer.

Miguel and the old Texas Ranger had become fast friends in the days after the shootout at the bazaar, at least as much as possible with the youngster not communicating all that well.

Throckmorton had put aside his inherent prejudice against brown-skinned people for the moment and taken the child under his leathery wing, buying him candy and video games, fretting over him. Miguel stayed close to the old lawman as we made our way out of Dallas, standing next to him as the Texas Ranger gassed up his Suburban, following him through the aisles of various convenience stores.

Maybe the boy needed a grizzled grandfather figure in his life. Maybe Aloysius Throckmorton, childless and lonely, felt a need to nurture.

"He still not talking?" Throckmorton asked.

I shook my head. "Why the urgency to get together?"

Several elderly men in overalls and gimme caps shuffled across the room. When they were past our table, Throckmorton said, "The police got a usable fingerprint off the gun that killed Fito."

A knot formed in my stomach. I'd wiped down the gun, but with the head injury and general chaos, I obviously hadn't done a very thorough job.

"A child's fingerprint," he said. "Not in any databases."

The waitress strolled over, asked if we wanted anything to eat. I ignored the rising nausea and ordered, because it seemed like the thing to do, huevos rancheros for both Miguel and me. Throckmorton asked for huevos con chorizo, heavy on the chorizo.

After she left, I said, "So they know about him now."

"They know about a kid, not him specifically."

The building had been empty when the killings occurred, so no one had heard the gunfire. Quinn Vega had helped me carry Javier to the office—I had the vaguest recollection of this—and place him on the sofa in the reception area, Miguel following us in a daze.

"They're still trying to put the hard drive for the video system back together," he said. "Good call, smashing it up."

I nodded, the memory of destroying the DVR fuzzy, like so many things from that night.

"What about Pecky Ruibal?" I asked. "Any leads on that?"

"That's a grade-five shitstorm. The assistant manager at the club, one of the other guys who got killed, his uncle's a state senator. Every investigator not working the Aztec Bazaar is logging overtime on the Ruibal case."

The waitress returned with a basket of chips and a bowl of salsa. Miguel ate a couple. Then he crossed his arms like he was cold and stared across the room.

"You know a place called Mendoza's Auto Salvage?" Throckmorton asked. "Over on West Davis by the highway?"

I shook my head, tried to keep a poker face.

In the aftermath of the shooting, I had been left with very few options. I'd been suffering from a head injury and not functioning at full speed. Even under those circumstances, my main goal remained crystal clear—protect Miguel.

So I'd decided to take a chance and call Throckmorton, being upfront with him about the situation at the Aztec Bazaar. Fito was dead, as were others. I didn't say who had pulled what trigger, and he didn't ask.

Confiding in a Texas Ranger nearing retirement—one who wanted nothing more than to stop the Vaqueros by whatever means necessary—seemed like a better idea than coming clean to the Dallas police. But I hadn't told him anything about Quinn Vega and me shooting the ponytailed man and the thug at the salvage yard.

"How about a guy named Gusano?" he asked. "Hooked up with the Mexican Mafia."

"The Worm?" I wondered if Throckmorton was about to slap the cuffs on me for murder.

"Not my first choice of nicknames." He paused. "You know him?"

I shook my head again, grateful I'd disposed of my weapon.

"Somebody took him out at the salvage yard. Ballistics matched the gun used in the other killings."

"Was Gusano's name on the list?" I asked. "His real name?"

Throckmorton shook his head.

Then he told me what I already knew. The fire at the warehouse that destroyed a car similar to the one witnessed at Pecky Ruibal's crime scene. The other two dead guys in the office, lower-echelon soldiers with the Mexican Mafia, killed with a different weapon, a Glock 9mm.

"Eleven murders in one day," he said. "Everybody at the Dallas PD is a teensy bit uptight, as you can imagine."

Eleven killings was a relatively quiet Saturday in Chicago. But in Texas, a Sunbelt state with historically low crime rates, that level of carnage made for lurid headlines and lots of official hand-wringing, police brass fearing for their jobs, government officials grandstanding for the news cameras.

I didn't say anything.

Seven of the murders had been committed by the same gun, the weapon used to kill Alejandro Sandoval, the crime that had started my involvement. Seven killings that I still didn't know anything about, despite my best efforts.

The circumstances surrounding the other four, the people who had died at the Aztec Bazaar, I was all too familiar with.

"You think there were two shooters?" I asked, hoping I sounded like I didn't know the answer.

He nodded.

"Maybe one of the Mexican Mafia soldiers is our killer," I said. "He and Gusano mixed it up and both caught a bullet. That would make the most sense."

"Maybe. Except the police didn't find any weapons at the scene."

I drummed my fingers on the tabletop, trying to look pensive and not worried.

"Somebody cleaned up," he said. "Took the guns, destroyed the DVR."

Neither of us spoke for a few moments.

"You used to carry a Glock, didn't you?" he asked.

"What's your point?"

"Nothing." He shrugged. "You always were a rebel."

The Texas Rangers were as tradition-bound and stuck in their ways as an eighty-year-old spinster living alone with a bunch of cats. Rangers wore the same garb—Stetsons and western-style shirts. Carried the same guns—Colt Government Models in ornately tooled holsters. Deviations were noticed, frowned upon.

The waitress brought our food.

Throckmorton dug in. Miguel picked at his. I just stared at the plate.

"You OK?" Throckmorton asked. "Something wrong with your eggs?"

I ate a bite, feigning enthusiasm. "Why'd you tell me to ditch the phone?"

"Ross's making noise about you being a person of interest. He knows you and me are friends. If he decides to check out my phone records . . ." He arched his eyebrows.

As a former homicide investigator, I actually felt a little sorry for Detective Ross. He had a morgue full of murder victims and precious little to go on.

Despite the fact that I had broken Fito's nose in a crowded bar, no one had admitted to the police that they'd seen either of us. Good for me in terms of the Dallas PD, bad in the sense that Fito's people knew I was there and that I had to have some knowledge of what happened to him.

All Ross had to go on, however, was the four dead bodies in Maria's store, an unidentified child's fingerprint, and no video.

I had talked to the detective by phone the next day, my head bandaged and aching like I'd drunk a bottle of tequila the night before.

I told him I was at my motel during the time Fito had been killed. With no cooperating witnesses or video, he couldn't very well contradict me. Also, it was common knowledge that I didn't handle security at night. That was the job of the patrol service, who mercifully was not on-site at the time.

Throckmorton stared across the room like he didn't want to look me in the eye.

I waited, knowing there was more to come.

"Ross's heard about Miguel," he said. "The partial fingerprint. You can imagine how his mind's working."

The youngster ate another couple of bites and stopped, looking back and forth between the two adults at the table.

I pushed away my plate, my mind worrying over logistics: how much money I had easy access to, where we could go next, the difficulty of getting Miguel a forged identity.

The waitress came over and asked if we needed anything else. Throckmorton shook his head. She cleared the table and left.

"How much longer you got on the job?" I asked.

"About to start using up vacation time now."

My only ally was days away from retirement.

Then it would be Miguel and me alone, facing Ross and his homicide investigation and an angry drug cartel.

- CHAPTER THIRTY-FOUR -

Outside the restaurant, Throckmorton and I stood by the side of his Suburban. Miguel was in my pickup.

"How many killings is that with the same gun?" I asked.

He mumbled to himself for a moment, tapping on his fingers with his thumb. "Six or seven, at least. Not counting the collateral damage at the club."

"Our guy's likely not a professional," I said. "Otherwise, he would have ditched the weapon after the first couple of hits."

He shrugged. "Maybe he was sending a message by using the same piece."

"Maybe. Maybe not. Sandoval at the tire store. A single round in the head would have been enough. But three times? One in the knee, for Pete's sake—that's like he wanted it to hurt."

Neither of us spoke. Cicadas screeched in the trees, and a truck hauling a gooseneck trailer lumbered down the road.

"You talked to Quinn Vega lately?" he asked.

I shook my head.

We'd spoken several times by phone in the week after the killings, but I hadn't communicated with her since Miguel and I had gone underground.

Witnessing Fito's death had seemed to calm her nerves.

In the immediate aftermath, she was no longer shaky and fearful. She'd found an ice pack for my head after I'd carried Javier to the office, helped me hold the phone while I called Throckmorton, propped me up as everything went woozy again.

"You thought about what to do now?" he asked. "I got a guy in Abilene who can put you up for a while."

"And then what?" I said.

Sooner or later, Throckmorton would run out of guys who were willing to hide me from the police and a drug cartel.

He rubbed the bridge of his nose like he was tired and reached inside his SUV, removing the picture by the speedometer.

"Me and my wife, you know we never had children."

I gave a half nod, half shrug.

He held up the photo. "This is my niece. My sister's kid."

"Looks like a nice girl."

"Smart, too. She was studying architecture at UT."

I decided not to comment on his use of the past tense.

"Unfortunately, she had a bad picker when it came to men."

"What happened?"

"Boyfriend was hooked up with one of the cartels, thought he was Scarface. Got her working as a mule, running shit across the bridge in Brownsville."

I understood now why he had helped me escape from the Aztec Bazaar, why he wasn't going to arrest me no matter how much jeopardy that choice put him in.

"She's in the penitentiary. Just turned twenty-six years old." He shook his head. "What do you think it's like for a pretty girl like her on the inside?"

I wondered if he was ever part of any DEA task force. Had all this started as a way for him to avenge what had happened to his niece?

That made as much sense as anything. We were all trying to fix something, to patch the cracks in our souls.

He returned the picture to its spot in his Suburban, and neither of us spoke for a few moments.

"Far as I can tell," I said, "there's only one way out."

He cocked his head.

"Give the Vaqueros the shooter. Negotiate a peace."

"That could work." He rubbed his chin.

"But that's back to square one. Because I still don't know who the killer is."

We returned to silence, staring at the ground.

He looked up. "Did you know that Quinn Vega's husband represented several people affiliated with the Vaqueros?"

"So I heard." I remembered the predicament Vega had found himself in with Pax Larson-Ibarra.

At his core, Frank Vega was an angry man, one with money and access to firearms. And the legal skills to stay under the radar of the police.

"Wouldn't it be funny if he were the killer?" Throckmorton chuckled.

• • •

Before I did anything else, I wanted to talk to Javier. He knew Frank Vega better than I did. He'd be able to give me a read on the man. Plus, I had the niggling feeling in the back of my mind that Javier hadn't been completely forthright with me about what he knew regarding the murders.

According to Throckmorton, he'd quit drinking. After waking up the next morning to a horde of homicide investigators tramping around the bazaar and no memory of the night before, Javier had decided enough was enough—rock bottom and all that.

So he'd checked in to a rehab facility, a thirty-day inpatient program in Fort Worth, leaving the running of the business to his CPA and a trusted cousin.

Throckmorton got into his Suburban and sped off down the road, disturbing a pair of buzzards feeding on a mangled pile of roadkill. If I were superstitious, I'd say that was some kind of omen. But I wasn't, so I joined Miguel in the old pickup, and together we headed east to Fort Worth.

An hour and a half later, I parked in a visitor slot in front of a one-story redbrick building a few blocks south of downtown, near the hospital district.

The place looked like a moderately successful law office, fresh paint on the trim, well-kept landscaping, nice cars in the parking area.

A sign on the glass entry doors read, THE ROSEDALE FACILITY.

Miguel and I stepped inside.

The entryway was decorated in soft pastels like the lobby of a Ramada Inn. A woman in her forties with spiky blonde hair sat at a desk facing the doors.

"Hi." I smiled, tried to look friendly.

No response.

"My name is Arlo Baines. I'd like to visit Javier Morales."

One of her eyebrows rose a quarter of an inch.

She opened a drawer, pulled out a single sheet of paper. She ran her finger down a list of some sort, lips pursed.

"You're his emergency contact." She frowned. "But your phone number doesn't work anymore."

"Switched carriers. I needed unlimited data."

She returned the paper to the drawer. "He's gone. I'm sorry."

Miguel stiffened beside me.

"Gone?" I said. "What the hell are you talking about?"

"He's left us."

I didn't speak, trying to get my head around what she was saying.

"He checked out early." She paused. "Against doctors' recommendation."

Miguel and I glanced at each other.

I turned my attention back to the woman. "When was this?"

"A little over a week ago."

I swore.

"Are you OK?" she asked.

"I'm fine. Just surprised."

"People who seek help here have an endless capacity to surprise." She opened another drawer, pulled out a packet of papers. "Would you like a brochure about our program?"

I shook my head and headed toward the door.

• • •

Outside in the pickup, I turned on the AC while Miguel buckled his seat belt.

"We have to go back to Dallas," I said.

He stared outside.

"Tenemos que ir a Dallas." I repeated myself in Spanish.

After a moment, he nodded.

"I know that you don't want to go there again. But we have to finish this."

"Sí." He spoke for the first time that day. "Finish it."

- CHAPTER THIRTY-FIVE -

I drove straight to Javier's house on Edgefield, circling the block a couple of times, looking for anything out of the ordinary.

It was early afternoon, a Tuesday. Everything appeared normal. The temperature was in the midnineties, so not many people outside. Only a few cars were on the street, all unoccupied.

I parked in Javier's driveway.

The grass was overgrown, the shades drawn. No different from any other day.

The neighbor to the north was working on a VW in his driveway. After a moment, he went inside, so Miguel and I exited the pickup.

I tried Javier's front door. Locked. We walked around to the back, checked that door. The same. I headed for Torres's place to the south, Miguel following me.

The old marine was lounging on a glider on the front porch, deep in the shadows, sipping from a can of Schlitz.

I stopped at the bottom of the steps and greeted him. He told us to come up and sit a spell.

Miguel and I climbed our way to the porch.

"*Cómo estás*, Miguel?" He smiled at the youngster. "You want to go see a movie?"

No answer.

The smile slowly disappeared. He looked at me, head cocked.

"Probably best that you don't mention we're in town," I said.

He nodded. "The boy, is he all right?"

"All things considered, yeah. Any idea where Javier is?"

He put his beer on the porch and stood. "You know that joint on Singleton next to the thrift shop?"

"Rudy's?"

"That's the one. He hangs out there, from what I hear."

I sighed, not liking the fact that my friend was spending time at an establishment that sold liquor.

Especially one like Rudy's, which was rough even by the standards of shithole bars in bad parts of town, the kind of place where the cockroaches had rap sheets.

Last year, a loan shark named Kel stabbed his mother at the bar and shoved her under the pool table, letting her bleed out. The pool players, one of whom was Kel's sister, never stopped their game. Just your typical Monday morning at Rudy's.

Torres took a step toward Miguel, smiling again. "You want to hang out for a while? Watch some TV?"

Miguel moved backward, wary.

Torres looked at me, his expression puzzled, bordering on worried.

"Thanks for all you've done," I said.

"I'm here if you need me."

I nodded, not wanting to say that we wouldn't be seeing him again.

• • •

Rudy's occupied a windowless cinder block building, the exterior walls covered in black paint that was fading to gray.

I parked between Javier's pickup and a thirty-year-old Pontiac with a bumper sticker that read GET THE US OUT OF THE UNITED NATIONS!

The Pontiac's engine was running, the windows up, a guy with a bushy white beard behind the wheel, asleep or passed out.

Miguel got out of the pickup before I could tell him not to.

I met him at the entrance. "Stay close, OK?"

He nodded, and I pushed open the door.

The interior of Rudy's smelled like bleach and beer and stale marijuana smoke. An old Marvin Gaye song, "Sexual Healing," played on the jukebox.

The bar itself sat in the back of the room and looked like it was made from painted plywood. Naugahyde booths, duct-taped to repair the cracks, lined the sidewalls, a pool table in the middle of the concrete floor.

In a booth on the right, a heavyset woman in her forties was making out with a guy half her age and weight. The woman wore a halter top and denim cutoffs. The guy had on a sailor suit but no shoes or socks.

The bartender was slicing lemons, using a long-bladed knife with a red grip and the surface of the bar as a cutting board. He stopped what he was doing and watched as Miguel and I entered the room.

It didn't take long to spot Javier, the only other person in the place.

He was in a booth on the other side of the pool table from the odd couple. He sat facing the door, reading a paperback, a coffee mug in front of him. He looked good, better than I'd ever seen him. His face was no longer puffy, skin tone a healthy pink instead of the gray pallor I'd grown used to.

I approached him. Miguel skipped ahead of me.

Javier closed the book. "I wondered when you two would be back."

Miguel smiled, slid next to him on the booth.

He hugged the boy, ruffled his hair. Miguel wrapped his arms around Javier's neck, a look of contentment on his face I hadn't seen in a long time.

"What are you doing in this place?" I asked.

"I come here and read." He held up the book, a Spanish-language version of a Sidney Sheldon novel. "No one disturbs me here."

"You ever thought about a library or a coffee shop?"

Silence.

I sat across from him. "We went to Fort Worth first. To visit you." Even to my own ears, the words sounded reproachful.

"You want me to make amends?" he asked. "That's one of the steps, you know. To say how sorry you are."

I didn't reply. Unlike his new, healthy appearance, his tone sounded familiar. Angry. Self-righteous. A pity party in the making.

He tapped the cup. "Coffee only. Satisfied?"

The jukebox switched songs, something twangy about divorce.

"We need to talk," I said.

He ignored me, turning his attention to Miguel. "*Qué tal, mijito?* You've grown. Hardly recognize you."

The youngster smiled. He opened his mouth like he was going to say something but didn't speak.

"What?" Javier raised his eyebrows in mock astonishment. "You can't even say hello to your old friend?"

No answer.

Javier looked at me, frowning.

"He doesn't talk much anymore," I said.

"What do you mean?"

"How much do you remember from that night?"

"Very little." His expression turned wistful. "Mostly the drinks. One after another."

I told him about Fito and Pax coming into the bar, how Fito wanted to purchase the entire operation but I cut short the negotiation by breaking his nose.

"You were in pretty bad shape," I said. "Quinn helped you leave. I followed a little later."

At the mention of someone assisting him, Javier stared into the coffee mug.

"I was going to get Miguel," I said. "You'd left him with Maria. But Fito and his buddy were waiting for us."

He looked up.

"They knew where I'd go. They used the front entrance to circle around."

He frowned, the look on his face indicating he didn't understand or didn't want to.

"They had the boy." I spoke the words slowly, carefully.

He didn't say anything. He took a sip of coffee, still frowning.

"Maria was part of it from the beginning," I said.

"I didn't know." He shook his head. "I left him there so I could get drunk. That's what I am, a drunk."

His voice sounded mechanical and dull, the words delivered by rote.

He turned his attention to Miguel. "Did they hurt you?"

Tears welled in the youngster's eyes. He looked back and forth between us.

"It's OK," I said. "You don't have to talk about it if you don't want to."

He rubbed his nose with one hand, sniffling.

"What happened after that?" Javier leaned forward. "How did it go down?"

I wondered how much he should know. He was as close to Miguel as I was. Maybe closer because of their shared heritage. Didn't that mean he had a right to know what happened? Shouldn't he know who had killed Fito?

Some things were better left unsaid.

"I don't remember much, either." I shrugged. "Took a pretty bad rap on the noggin."

He stared at my forehead. "But you killed Fito, and that's what counts."

I didn't correct him.

He slid one hand under Miguel's chin, tilting his head up, peering into his eyes.

"*Lo siento,*" he said. "I'm sorry."

The boy smiled.

"Have you talked to Frank Vega lately?" I asked.

Javier turned his attention my way, face blank. "Why would I talk to him?"

"A bunch of people got killed in his building. I figured he might have something to say about that."

"I'm going to sell the business," Javier said. "El Corazón Roto and the *mercado*. Everything."

For some reason, this news didn't surprise me.

I was about to ask if he had a buyer in mind, but I saw the bartender pick up a cell phone and move to a spot behind the bar as far away from us as possible.

He punched in a number and held the phone to his ear, glancing our way while doing a poor job of trying to look like he wasn't interested in us.

"Who's he calling?" I asked.

Javier turned toward the bar. He spoke without looking back, his voice low. "You should get away from this place. Leave the boy here. I'll look after him."

The sailor had passed out, his face resting on the tabletop. The woman was rummaging through his wallet. She glanced at the bartender, then at us. She stuffed a wad of cash in her halter top and left.

"They're looking for you," Javier said. "The Vaqueros. They want revenge for Fito."

A knot formed in my stomach.

The bartender's call ended. He looked at our booth, not trying to hide his interest anymore.

"They ask about the Texas Ranger." Javier paused. "I'm sorry, Arlo. Truly I am."

"For what?"

"That I got you into this mess."

If anybody had gotten me into anything, it was Throckmorton. But that really wasn't true, either, I realized, finally grasping that I'd walked into this of my own accord.

"You didn't force me to do anything."

I liked to think that I was trying to protect Miguel, but that was only part of it. I had a need to repair problems that were better left alone, to fix the unfixable.

Maybe that was the cop in me. Or maybe I was trying to make my own sort of amends to those I had lost.

When all this started, it would have been so easy just to leave town with the boy. That would have been the smart move. But I chose a different path. And here I was, sitting in a joint where even the rats were armed, worrying about getting killed by an angry drug cartel.

"I can't stop thinking about my wife and little girls," Javier said. "They stay in my dreams. Always there, calling for me."

I looked away from the bartender. It was time to leave, but I didn't move.

"That day we met. You should have left me alone," he said.

I realized that he was talking about how I had stopped him from committing suicide, an action I felt relatively sure wasn't part of the program at the Rosedale Facility.

"You need to go back to Fort Worth," I said. "Or talk to a counselor. Or something."

He rubbed the bridge of his nose, brow furrowed.

"Why is it so easy for you?" he asked. "My family, they're gone, but they won't leave me alone. At night I hear their voices. It's like I can feel their tears."

Underneath the anger and the sadness, Javier was jealous of me, which was baffling. Did he think I wasn't still grieving? Was I better able to hide my pain? To mask the suffering?

He shook his head. "I'm sorry, Arlo. I'm going to make this right, I promise."

I wanted to ask him what he meant. I had trouble imagining what he could do to help the situation.

"You need to leave, though," he said. "Right now."

Before I could stand, the bartender approached our table.

"You want something to drink? Coffee or a beer?" He smiled at me awkwardly, trying to look like this wasn't the first time anyone had ever been offered table service at Rudy's.

"How long before they get here?" I asked.

He frowned. "What are you talking about?"

"The call you just made. How long before somebody arrives?"

"I don't understand." He enunciated each syllable with great care.

Acting was not his forte. The look on his face indicated he understood perfectly, eyes wide and innocent.

"Give me your phone." I held out my hand. "I want to talk to them."

"Look, buddy. I'm just a bartender. I don't know what you're getting at."

I slid out of the booth and threw him to the ground, cranking his arm up behind his back. If I'd had cuffs, I would have used them. Instead, I reached in his pocket with my free hand and pulled out a cell phone.

Underneath me, he bucked, trying to free himself.

"What's the passcode?" I asked.

No answer.

I raised his arm a notch.

He rattled off a string of numbers, the address of the bar.

As I entered the digits, the front door opened.

- CHAPTER THIRTY-SIX -

There were two of them.

Latino men in their twenties, tattooed up like the guy who'd been with Fito. Local muscle if I had to guess, members of some gang who had affiliated themselves with the Vaqueros, getting their shot at the big time.

The bartender started bucking again. "Get him off me. I did what your guy wanted."

They flanked out.

I stuck the phone in my pocket, debating whether to pull my gun.

Problem was, I didn't want to shoot anybody. I was tired of death, the shock waves sent out into the larger world from someone's passing. Even a pair of lowlifes like these two.

So I rolled off the bartender and lunged for the pool table, grabbing a cue stick.

The one closest to me reached under his shirt.

I swung the heavy end of the stick at his skull. He jumped back, and the wood missed his head.

He backpedaled, pulling a gun from his waistband.

I took two quick steps forward and jabbed the end of the stick into his face, aiming for his nose.

I missed again. Squished an eye instead, dead center.

He yelped and dropped the gun, hands going to his face as he collapsed to the floor.

Before I could do anything else, a blast of fire erupted against the small of my back.

I fell, too, dropping my stick, disoriented. I looked up from the floor to see the second hood holding another pool cue.

He cocked the stick over one shoulder like it was a baseball bat and he was Babe Ruth, the ball in this instance being my head.

No debate this time.

I fumbled for my gun, moving much too slowly. I wasn't going to reach the weapon in time.

Everything moved in slow motion.

The hood's mouth twisted into a frown. His nostrils flared; the muscles in his shoulders bunched. The wood circled from behind his back, headed toward my skull.

I raised an arm to stop the blow, risking a broken bone rather than another head trauma.

But the blow never came.

The hood stopped swinging.

The stick slid from his grasp, clattered on the floor.

He struggled to reach behind his back, to a point between his shoulder blades.

After a couple of seconds, he dropped to his knees. Then he fell forward, propping himself up by one hand, the other grasping for the red-handled knife sticking in his back.

Miguel stood behind him, staring at the dying man with the same cold eyes I'd last seen when he'd shot Fito.

I got to my feet, back throbbing, gun finally in my hand.

Javier was still in the booth, mouth hanging open.

The bartender dashed behind the bar, heading toward the landline by the cash register.

I aimed at the phone, a cordless unit mounted on the wall, maybe twenty feet away. I squeezed the trigger. The gun fired, the noise loud in the low-ceilinged room. The bullet hit the handset somewhere in the bottom half. Bits of plastic scattered.

The bartender raised his hands, face white, arms trembling.

I shifted my aim to the man's head. "Put your keys on the bar."

He didn't respond, his breathing shallow and rapid.

"The keys to your vehicle," I said. "Do it."

He reached into his pocket and tossed a key ring on the bar.

"Now get out," I said. "Start running down Singleton. If I see you when I leave, I'll shoot you in both knees."

The man gulped, eyes wide. After a moment, he dashed out of the bar.

Javier slid from the booth, limbs shaking. He stared at Miguel.

"Where's Frank Vega?" I asked.

"Have you lost your mind?"

I didn't speak, unsure of the answer.

"What have you done to the boy? He just stabbed someone."

"I took care of him," I said. "While you were off getting drunk."

Words have power—at least those did. He blinked several times, staggered back like a strong wind was blowing against him.

I felt sorry for what I had said as soon as the words left my mouth. But I wasn't going to say so, suddenly aware of the anger and resentment that had built up because of his actions.

"You have to leave town," he said. "They're not giving up until they find you."

"Do I look like the running kind?" I stuck the gun back in my waistband.

"Take Miguel with you. I'll send money. Just get out of Dallas."

The hood with the damaged eye crawled to a corner of the room, one hand held to his face.

Miguel grabbed the hood's gun from the floor and checked the chamber for a live round. He handled the weapon like a seasoned veteran, his movements assured, no wasted effort. Satisfied the pistol was ready to fire, he flicked on the safety and stuck it in his waistband.

"Where did you learn to do that?" Javier asked.

No answer.

Javier turned to me. "Stay away from Frank Vega. You don't want to be involved."

"Involved in what?"

"Promise me, Arlo. Promise me you will leave town."

I headed toward the door where Miguel waited for me. I was done making promises.

- CHAPTER THIRTY-SEVEN -

I walked toward the old pickup, my back throbbing, sweat trickling down my face.

The bartender was nowhere to be seen, but the passed-out drunk was still in the Pontiac. Overhead, a jet streaked across a chrome-colored sky, headed to parts unknown.

The thought of driving down some dirt road with no destination filled my mind, just the boy and me.

Miguel ran ahead of me. He opened the passenger door and jumped in. A moment later, I slid behind the wheel.

The hooker who'd been inside walked around the corner of the building.

She stared at me as I cranked the ignition. She knew what kind of vehicle we were in, meaning the Vaqueros would too in the not-too-distant future. The police would as well, probably, a BOLO going out for the elderly pickup and the young Latino male who was a suspect in a bar stabbing.

I slid the transmission into gear, jammed on the gas, and raced out of the lot. As I drove, I unlocked the bartender's phone and handed it to Miguel, telling him to Google Frank Vega's office address.

Twenty minutes later, I parked in front of a Victorian-style house in a gentrified neighborhood north of downtown. The home was wood sided, with ornate trim above a wide front porch, the exterior walls turquoise with light-gold accents. A sign in the front yard read LAW OFFICES OF FRANK VEGA.

The structure was at least a century old but in immaculate condition, similar to the other places on the street, at one point homes but now converted into offices.

I asked Miguel to give me the gun he'd taken from the gangbanger back at the bar.

After what he'd been through, I figured it wasn't the smartest move to leave him with a weapon. He handed over the pistol without hesitating. I stuck the gun in the other side of my waistband and told him to stay in the truck; I wouldn't be long.

He nodded but didn't speak, his expression trusting.

I took the steps leading to the porch two at a time.

The front door was made from heavy glass and wrought iron, offering a view of an entryway with polished hardwood floors and stark-white walls.

I rang the bell.

No movement from within, so I tried the knob.

The door opened, so I stepped inside.

The place seemed empty. To the left was what appeared to be the old living room, now a reception area. A desk with a computer and a phone facing a leather sofa and a coffee table.

Across from the reception area was the old dining room, partially obscured by a large sliding door halfway open.

From my vantage point, I could see a desk covered with files as well as several diplomas on the far wall.

Frank's office.

I stepped inside.

The room was empty.

I searched the rest of the building, another two offices that had furniture but appeared to be unoccupied, and a kitchen at the rear that looked out over a backyard and an empty garage.

A coffee maker sat by the sink, the carafe half-full of hot coffee.

I found a mug in the cabinet, poured myself a cup, and headed back to the front office.

Maybe Frank was grabbing a late lunch somewhere, his receptionist having stepped out for a moment.

I sat behind his desk, took a sip of coffee, and pulled the bartender's cell phone from my pocket.

The last number dialed had a local area code.

As soon as I pressed "Redial," I heard the back door open, followed by footsteps on the old hardwood. The footsteps grew louder as a phone rang in two places—my ear from the bartender's cell and down the hall in the direction of whoever was approaching.

I yanked the cell away from my head and stared at the number. The ringing down the hall continued. I ended the call.

The ringing down the hall stopped.

I stood, grabbed my pistol.

Frank Vega appeared in the doorway, a phone in his hand.

"The bartender was reaching out to you," I said.

He nodded. "You've been busy, haven't you?"

"You're working for the Vaqueros?" I dropped the phone on his desk like it was hot. Nothing made sense.

"I thought you were smart," he said. "To be real honest, I'm not seeing that right now."

I tried to fathom what was unfolding in front of me. Frank Vega was part of the organization?

"Put the gun down," he said.

215

I didn't move.

"We've got the kid." He stepped into the room.

I looked out the window. My pickup was empty, Miguel nowhere to be seen.

Another figure appeared in the doorway, a Latino man in a navy-blue polo shirt, a wine-colored birthmark on one cheek.

Pax Larson-Ibarra.

"So this is the great Arlo Baines," he said.

"Where's Miguel?" I asked.

Frank Vega smiled. "He's with us now. And so are you."

- CHAPTER THIRTY-EIGHT -

My fingers hurt from gripping the pistol so hard.

I aimed at Frank's chest, my breathing shallow.

"Drop the gun," he said. "Last thing you want to do is shoot me."

I didn't move.

"This boy you're so fond of," Pax said. "Miguel. Do you want us to hurt him?"

Fear clawed at my belly, my skin clammy.

"You think he's bluffing?" Frank asked. "I promise you, he's not."

I lowered the pistol. After a moment, I placed it on the desk.

"A wise decision." Frank pulled out his mouse gun, pointed the muzzle at me.

Pax removed the other gun from my waistband and zip-tied my hands behind my back. Then he led me out the rear to the navy-blue Suburban with Mexican license plates. He put me in the cargo area next to a bound and gagged Miguel, the boy's eyes fearful. Pax slid a black hood over my head, and everything disappeared.

I tried not to panic, not to second-guess my decision to take the gun from Miguel.

A moment later, the hatch slammed closed. A couple of seconds after that, I heard the passenger doors shut, felt movement as the SUV backed out of the driveway.

Then there was nothing but the hum of tires on asphalt.

I tried to keep track of the turns and the time elapsed, but that works only in the movies.

After a short period, a phone rang, and a muffled conversation ensued.

I could hear Frank's voice, angry, but I couldn't understand the words, except for the last few: *Hire some more people, then.*

He swore, and the SUV made an abrupt turn, throwing my body into Miguel's. The vehicle sped up, pushing us both toward the rear of the cargo area.

I wondered what had happened. What new bit of information arrived in that phone call? What kind of people did he need to hire?

No more talking from the front. As the SUV continued its journey, I whispered to Miguel that everything would be OK, telling him we'd get out of this somehow. He didn't respond.

A while later—maybe fifteen minutes, maybe thirty—the SUV stopped, and the cargo hatch opened.

Somebody grabbed my arms, pulled me out.

Wherever we were, it was hot, sun beating down on the black cloth over my head.

"Miguel?" I said, straining to hear.

No answer. Just the muffled stuffiness of the hood.

"Walk." Pax's voice in my ear.

Hands guided me.

The *whoosh* of a door, the air cooler.

Even through the hood, I recognized the smell.

El Corazón Roto.

Someone pushed me over, and I fell on my side with a *thud*. The footsteps departed, and there was only silence.

"Miguel?" I whispered. "Can you hear me?"

No response.

I maneuvered myself to my knees, harder than it sounds with bound hands and unseeing eyes. I tried unsuccessfully to shake off the hood.

After a moment, I sat down cross-legged and waited.

A period of time passed. Maybe ten minutes. Maybe more.

Another set of footsteps approached, different from before. Lighter, more clipped.

Everything turned white as someone yanked away the hood.

I blinked, vision slowly returning.

Quinn Vega stood in front of me. She wore a pair of jeans, a silk blouse, and the boots she'd bought weeks before at the Aztec Bazaar.

I looked around.

The place was empty except for the two of us.

No bartender, no customers, no Frank or Pax.

And no Miguel.

"Are you OK?" she asked.

The tables and chairs were gone, as were the bottles of liquor behind the bar. The booths along the wall, attached to the floor, remained. A pile of construction equipment lay stacked in the back of the room—ladders and drop cloths, buckets of paint, sawhorses.

"We're remodeling," she said. "Place needs freshening."

That answered the question of who was buying the businesses.

"Where's the boy?" I asked.

"Get up so I can cut you loose." She pulled a folding knife from her back pocket.

I stared at her but didn't move.

"I'm not going to hurt you," she said.

I stood, turned my back to her. A moment later, my hands were free. I rubbed my wrists, trying to get the circulation flowing again.

She pointed to a booth. "Let's sit down."

"Miguel. Where is he?"

"He's safe. I promise you that."

I eyed the knife still in her hand, debating my chances.

"Don't." She folded the blade, slid it into her pocket. "Guards are just outside."

I didn't speak. I tried to keep my face blank, my intentions hidden. I was close enough that I could throat-punch her and take the weapon, but that wouldn't help me find Miguel.

Still, the idea of Quinn Vega lying on the floor, struggling to breathe through her ruined trachea, had a certain appeal.

"I'm sorry it's come to this," she said. "Really, I am."

"The story Frank told." I shook my head. "Pax and his nephew, all that was bullshit."

"Funny how people believe what they want to, isn't it?"

A few seconds passed as we both stared at each other.

"You were so oblivious." She chuckled. "High school all over again. I was the girl who needed protecting."

I didn't understand what she meant, and it must have showed on my face.

"You don't remember, do you? How you looked out for me." She sounded wistful, almost nostalgic. "It was a long time ago. Still, it makes me just a little bit sad that you forgot."

"Who spray-painted your garage?"

"Frank, of course. I told him not to shoot out the lock, but he never listens to me." She sat in a booth by the front door. "He has a flair for theatrics, being a trial lawyer and all."

She motioned for me to take the place across from her.

I didn't move.

"You're wondering why, aren't you?" she asked. "How come we picked you."

I took several deep breaths. Tried to stop the rage building in the pit of my stomach while the sequence of everything replayed in my head.

They had chosen me; that much was obvious. Frank asking if I would escort his wife through the Aztec Bazaar. Quinn telling me that Frank was in danger from the same people who had killed Sandoval. The made-up story about Pax. Quinn not wanting to be left alone.

"Why does anybody do anything?" I said. "Control."

"Very good." She nodded approvingly.

"You needed someone who could keep you informed about the murder investigations," I said. "You wanted to know if the police were getting close."

She nodded again. "We kept tabs on what Ross knew through you."

I remembered the stuff I'd told her, never dreaming she and her husband were working for the cartel and that the killings were internal.

"Were the murders at Mendoza's part of your plan, too?" I asked.

She shook her head. "There weren't supposed to be any witnesses to Pecky's killing, obviously. But we . . . Oh, let's just say there was some sloppiness on our end."

The money courier and singer, gunned down with two of his bandmates and a nightclub manager. Sloppiness indeed.

I forced myself not to react to her admission that an error, the first I was aware of, had occurred.

Everybody eventually made a mistake, especially in the nerve-racking business of killing people. But Quinn and Frank Vega had been extraordinarily lucky.

Until they weren't. Until there were witnesses. In this case the people on Pecky Ruibal's tour bus, the roadies and supporting musicians getting ready for Los Tres Reyes's gig at El Club de la Paloma.

Frank Vega had been using the black Prelude as transportation to and from the hits. A smart idea, using a nearly untraceable vehicle, storing the car at Gusano's chop shop.

But the people on the band's bus saw the Honda, which meant that Frank had to get rid of the car. And Gusano knew about the vehicle, which meant he was a loose end who had to die. Which led to the deaths of Gusano's associates. The snowball effect.

One error meant there would be more. A way to take them down.

I slid into the booth across from where she sat. It wouldn't be too hard to lean over the table and strangle the life out of her with my bare hands.

"Don't feel bad." She smiled. "You always were a sucker for the damsel-in-distress routine."

I debated how to respond, what to say that would keep the conversation going. The more she talked, the greater the odds that I could find out where Miguel was being held. Then I could kill her, get the boy, and leave.

Even as I thought about the series of events that needed to happen, I realized how futile that plan was.

One step at a time. Just keep her talking.

"How long have you and Frank been working for the Vaqueros?" I asked.

The anger returned to her eyes, along with a flash of irrationality, a mind coming unmoored from the banks of sanity.

She leaned across the table. "We're not working *for* the Vaqueros. We are the Vaqueros."

- CHAPTER THIRTY-NINE -

The business of Dallas was business, according to Quinn.

Commerce ruled.

The city served as a major corporate hub. Companies relocated to the area every year, drawn by the entrepreneurial-friendly environment, central location, and well-developed transportation network.

The last two were also reasons why the Vaqueros had come here, instead of, say, Austin or San Antonio. On a map, the metropolitan area composed of Fort Worth and Dallas looked like an enormous spider, one with thousands of legs, each a highway leading to the rest of the country.

Seventy-five percent of the illegal narcotics imported from Mexico came across the Texas border, the vast majority moving through the Dallas area, transported by secondary organizations who partnered with the Vaqueros.

If someone purchased a quarter ounce of pot in Chicago or Atlanta or Kansas City, or any point in between, the odds were good it had gone through Dallas. It was just a matter of time, Quinn explained, before the cartels expanded their reach, capturing the transportation routes north of the border.

Dallas was the logical choice for a base; any business consultant could have told you that. The city was operating in a vacuum, contraband-wise. Too many opportunities existed here for someone not to take advantage.

A law school classmate with a small practice in Brownsville had approached Frank a couple of years before, introducing him to Pax Larson-Ibarra, an energetic young man who was looking for investments in the North Texas area—real estate, small businesses, that sort of thing.

The money, Frank later learned, came from Pax's brother, a defrocked priest who earned his living in a manner that most people preferred not to discuss openly. Import-export, they might say with a shrug.

The source of the capital didn't bother Frank. Business was business. That was the Dallas way. He was a master of rationalization, according to Quinn, justifying whatever it took to make a buck.

Pax began to spend more and more time in Dallas, and pretty soon he and Frank became friends as much as business associates. They enjoyed the same things—good food, fast cars, pretty women. Quinn's eyes narrowed when she mentioned the last.

After a year or so, Pax approached Frank with another proposition.

Pax's brother was worried about a takeover by one of his lieutenants, the man in charge of the rapidly expanding Texas infrastructure, an infrastructure that Frank had helped put into place.

Would Frank help Pax and his brother to secure what was rightfully theirs, this burgeoning empire they had created?

It would be simple, really. They just needed to put their own people in place. Getting rid of the existing personnel was going to be messy, but the rewards would be worth any momentary discomfort Frank Vega might feel.

Intrigued, not to mention greedy, Frank asked just what kind of rewards they were talking about.

Pax told him the plan. His brother wanted to give Frank control of Texas, the entire state. What better person to handle their affairs than an attorney, an officer of the court?

The numbers were staggering, Quinn told me. How could anyone turn that down?

Frank didn't, of course, and the killings began.

• • •

A text message dinged.

Quinn reached into her back pocket and removed a phone, tapping out a reply.

"Sorry," she said. "Business is booming. A million details to take care of."

The message whooshed, sent on its way.

She looked up. "Where were we?"

"Talking about money," I said. "The root of all evil."

"How biblical. The priest would like that."

"Who was Fito?"

"He worked for the lieutenant Pax's brother was worried about," she said. "He was trying to stop the killings. Find out who was responsible."

Fito, Throckmorton, and I had obviously subscribed to the same theory: the murders were because a rival cartel was making a play for Vaquero territory. None of us had realized that the attacks were internal.

When Quinn and Frank had learned Fito was in town and why he was there, I could only imagine how strong their fear was, the sleepless nights, churning stomachs, jittery nerves.

Maybe only then did it sink in for them that they were playing an exceedingly dangerous game, wading into the middle of a drug cartel and staging a bloody coup. The outcome might have easily gone a different way, and they both would have ended up in a vat of acid.

"Why'd you tell me all this?" I asked.

"Didn't you want to know?" She paused. "Are you happy with the way your life's going, Arlo? Do you want to be a drifter forever?"

She shifted in her seat. Under the table, her leg brushed against mine, lingering a moment. Her eyes softened, and a faint smile appeared on her lips.

"Our business needs someone like you," she said. "I can pay you every month what you made in a year as a cop."

I looked across the room, trying to project the image that I was considering her offer. I wondered about her mental stability, if she really believed I'd work for her.

"You'd be spending time with me. I need someone I can trust to watch my back." She smiled. "We'd have a good time."

The way she spoke those last few words left no doubt in my mind as to what my other duties would entail. The idea of being Quinn Vega's side piece while working for her and her husband made me nauseous.

"Sounds interesting. What's the catch?"

"Why does there have to be a catch?"

Because there always is, I thought, *especially with people like you*.

She shrugged. "I just need someone who's not squeamish when it comes to getting his hands dirty."

"I'm not an assassin."

"Really?" She smirked, the crazy back in her eyes. "What about the people who killed your wife and children?"

The air caught in my throat, grief mixing with anger, a toxic cauldron bubbling just beneath the surface.

"I've read everything I could about that case," she said. "You were the only suspect until your father-in-law confessed. How convenient that he took the rap, right as his financial world crumbled."

I flexed my fingers, imagined them around her throat.

She tapped out a text.

A moment later, the exit door at the rear of the bar opened, and Stodghill the gun dealer approached our table, a large manila envelope in one hand. He was wearing the same tactical vest that he'd had on when Quinn and I had visited his place the month before.

I remembered Quinn worrying that he would recognize her from dealing with Frank, how Stodghill had acted like he'd never seen her before. Their performances had been Oscar-worthy. Amazing how well money can motivate a person.

"That was some *Donnie Brasco*–level work," I said. "Color me impressed."

They both shrugged, appearing satisfied.

I looked at Stodghill. "Shoulda figured a crooked son of a bitch like you would be involved in this."

He dropped the envelope on the table but didn't speak. The package was heavy, landing with a metallic *clank*.

I turned to Quinn and nodded in Stodghill's direction. "What's the payoff for our merchant-of-death friend?"

"He's moving his business to the bazaar," she said.

"We're going to have a separate storefront for the used guns." He crossed his arms. "Private-party transactions only."

Gun sales between two individuals didn't require the paperwork and background checks that a transaction with a licensed firearms dealer mandated. However, there were numerous ways a dealer could direct inventory to the used gun market.

"A ready supply of untraceable weapons." I nodded. "Just what every drug cartel needs."

"Speaking of weapons that are untraceable." Quinn dumped out the contents of the envelope, a pistol and a sheet of paper. "This one is very much traceable."

The paper appeared to be a copy of the ATF form required when someone buys a gun from a licensed dealer.

Quinn slid the document across the table so I could better see my name written in block letters.

I pointed to the gun. "That's my Glock, isn't it?"

The one I thought I had thrown into the river after the killings at Mendoza's salvage yard.

She nodded. "And this is the paperwork showing that gun being sold to you by our mutual acquaintance."

Stodghill grinned, and I added him to the list of people I wanted to throat-punch.

"At the river," Quinn said, "when you went to throw away the guns, I took this one out, stuck it in my overnight bag."

I remembered pulling off the road at the bridge, parking where the fishermen usually gathered. I'd walked around the truck to get the sack from Quinn's side. She must have removed the weapon in those few seconds.

She put the gun and the paper back into the manila envelope. She handed the envelope to Stodghill, who left the bar.

"Those go straight to Detective Ross if you don't do exactly as I tell you." She glared at me.

Neither of us spoke for a moment.

"I don't want to threaten Miguel," she said. "I know what he means to you."

I nodded. "That's probably best."

"But you need to know his safety depends on what you do next."

I waited. She had me, and she knew it. A double whammy—the boy and the gun.

"A couple of more loose ends that need taking care of," she said. "Then Texas is secure."

"You mean somebody who needs killing?"

She nodded.

"Who?"

"My husband," she said. "You're going to kill Frank."

- CHAPTER FORTY -

Quinn slid out of the booth.

"Why Frank?" I asked.

She strode to the front entrance. "Don't try anything. I have to send messages to keep the boy alive."

I stayed seated.

She stopped by the door, turned, and looked at me, head cocked.

I didn't move.

In a hostage situation, which this was, there were two primary goals.

Number one: try to escape as soon as possible. That didn't seem to be a reasonable option given the fact that they had Miguel as well as my tainted pistol.

That left the second goal: establish whatever control of the situation you can, by whatever means available.

"Get up," she said. "We're leaving."

"Not yet. Not until you fill me in."

Her eyes narrowed. "You think I'm screwing around here?"

The jeans she wore were slim fit, expensive looking. She had a knife in one back pocket, the cell phone in the other. The front pockets appeared empty, and her shirt was tucked in. All of which indicated that she didn't have a weapon other than the blade.

Maybe she'd been telling the truth weeks before at Stodghill's shop when she said she didn't like guns. Not the best attitude to have when you were in her line of work—like a carpenter who didn't care for hammers—but who was I to judge?

"If you want me to kill your husband," I said, "you need to tell me why."

She marched across the room, leaned on the table, face inches from mine. "Because I said so, that's why."

I could smell her sweat, see the pores of her skin. I didn't react.

A moment passed.

"You ever killed anybody?" I asked. "Other than the guy at Mendoza's?"

She blinked a couple of times but didn't speak, which was the answer I'd guessed—no.

"Tricky work, killing people." I paused. "A million things can go wrong."

She pushed herself off the table, crossed her arms.

"I need to know as much as possible up front," I said. "The location, what kind of security's there, who else is on the premises. Why this has to happen now."

She pursed her lips and stared at me.

"You don't want a repeat of Pecky Ruibal, do you?" I asked. "All those dead bodies at that nightclub."

After a moment, she shook her head.

I waited.

"This business doesn't take kindly to weakness," she said. "And Frank is a weak man."

I didn't speak, knowing there had to be more.

"The women," she said. "That's going to trip him up eventually."

She wanted me to believe her actions were not personal, but that was clearly not the case.

Jealousy wrapped up as a business decision.

Another mistake.

• • •

The main entrance to El Corazón Roto was unlocked, a tactical error considering there'd been a hostile inside with only one unarmed person as a guard.

I stepped outside before she reached the door, another small effort to exert control.

She didn't try to stop me. She just followed me out.

The sun was bright and hot.

There was no security that I could see, another bit of info that I stored away, right next to Frank Vega's overheard comment: *Hire some more people, then.*

Only a handful of vehicles were by the bar. Several pickups full of building materials and the late-model Mercedes sedan that had been parked in the Vega garage. Quinn's car.

Tuesday afternoon, the parking lot should be fuller than this.

"We shut down half the bazaar," she said. "Remodeling for our new tenants."

"Where's Miguel? I want to see him before we leave."

Despite the heat, the air between us seemed to grow cold as an icy expression formed on her face.

"You're done asking questions," she said. "If you stall one more time, I'll make a call and have somebody bring us one of the boy's fingers."

After a moment, I nodded. "Understood."

A small measure of tranquility settled over me at that moment as I realized that one way or the other, she was going to die today. Maybe I would as well, but not before killing her.

She handed me a key fob, pointed to the Mercedes. "You're driving."

I slid behind the wheel while she walked around to the passenger door.

The interior of the vehicle had been freshly cleaned, the dash shiny, the carpet vacuumed. A rolled-up yoga mat was in the rear next to a reusable grocery bag from Whole Foods.

I realized that for all of Quinn's bravado and tough talk, she had no clue what operating on the street was really like.

Once we were both inside, I said, "Where are we going?"

"My house."

I turned on the ignition, pulled out of the parking lot. "Who else is there?"

She glanced at me but didn't respond.

"I'm not stalling. I don't want to walk into a crew of cartel thugs."

"You won't have that problem, trust me."

Her voice held a faint trace of irony, and Frank's comment came back to me again. Were they running short on manpower? Could they have expanded too quickly?

"Only two people are there," she said. "Frank and Pax."

"Whose side is Pax on?"

No answer.

"I need to know if he's friend or foe."

"Pax recognizes weaknesses the same way I do," she said.

So the cartel connection was on board with taking out the new head of Texas. Maybe that had been the plan all along—use Frank to eliminate the lieutenant's people, then kill Frank once everything was wrapped up.

Quinn obviously hadn't completed all the calculations yet. She didn't realize that after one Vega was gone, it would be a simple matter to kill the second. Then Pax and his brother would control the territory themselves. Honorable men, these were not.

I didn't say any of that, of course. I just nodded, and we drove in silence for a while.

When we were about a mile away, I said, "Where's the gun?"

She pointed to the glove compartment.

I decided it was time to push her a little more.

"Why can't Pax handle this himself?" I asked.

She turned and stared at me.

"Don't you think Frank's going to be suspicious when I just show up at his house?"

She crossed her arms, looked out the window.

"You sure no one else is going to be there?" I asked.

If I were running a smuggling crew and someone brought an allegedly former enemy turned hit man into my home, you wouldn't be able to count the guns aimed at him.

She nodded.

"Running a lean operation, huh?"

"Quit talking and drive," she said.

They were short on personnel. The lack of guards. Only two people at their house.

The lieutenant they'd cut out was no doubt a street guy, which was how he came to be a lieutenant. He had the connections to the local gangs, knew how to control the troops, keep everything humming. Maybe they were hoping to take over those connections, but that hadn't happened yet. Maybe the connections figured they'd cut out Frank and Pax. Who knew?

A lot of variables. Buckets of mistakes.

I wondered about the two gangbangers at the bar, the one Miguel had knifed and the guy I'd jabbed in the eye. How many more were there? Also, how pissed were they at the boy and me right now?

One problem at a time.

We drove the rest of the way without talking. When we reached White Rock Lake, I pulled to the side of the road, her house a few hundred yards away.

"Time for the gun." I pointed to the glove compartment.

She didn't move.

"You own me," I said. "You really think I'm going to try anything?"

She stared at me, face blank, one eyelid twitching.

I shrugged. "Suit yourself, then. You can pull the trigger."

She took several deep breaths. Opened the glove compartment, removed a pistol, handed it to me.

The gun was a Beretta 9mm, at one time the standard issue for the US military. This one had a full magazine with a round in the chamber, but the serial number had been filed off.

I leaned forward, slipped the pistol in my waistband. "Where's Frank going to be?"

"In his office. The room next to where we met before."

She was referring to the sitting area with the picture window overlooking the lake, where they had spun their tale about Pax.

"And Pax is going to be with him?"

"I don't know." She sounded exasperated. "I don't keep track of him every second. He'll be in the house somewhere."

"Somewhere?"

"He's not going to interfere," she said. "What more do you want?"

Her voice sounded shrill and loud, like she was teetering on the edge of a breakdown.

I smiled a little on the inside and pulled away from the lake, turning a few moments later onto the Vega driveway.

The Maserati was parked by the front door, next to the navy-blue Suburban. In the distance, I could see the garage. All three doors were open, each space empty.

"How much bleach do you have?" I asked.

"What?"

"And towels." I paused. "For the cleanup."

Her face grew white.

"You forget Mendoza's already?" I said. "When people get shot, they bleed. It's a forensics nightmare."

She looked like she was going to say something, but the words wouldn't form, mouth opening and closing.

"Also, what's your plan for getting rid of the body?"

"What the hell do you mean, what's my plan?" She spluttered out the words. "That's what you're here for."

"Hey, I've only been on the job for thirty minutes." I parked behind the Maserati. "Hadn't really had time to line anything up."

Quinn muttered to herself and then turned to stare at her house, hands clenched into fists.

A few moments passed.

I turned off the ignition. "It's a hell of a thing, killing your spouse."

She glared at me.

"You may hate his guts," I said, "but he's still a part of you. You're still gonna feel a loss."

"I lost him a long time ago." She grasped the door handle but made no move to exit.

Another few seconds passed.

"You having second thoughts?" I asked.

She shook her head but continued to stare at the house.

I decided to turn up the pressure.

"You should know something about Miguel," I said.

"What?" She snapped out of her funk, looked at me.

"He has asthma. Really bad. Stress makes it worse. He needs medication."

She shifted in her seat, lips pressed together.

"I was on the way to the drugstore when Frank snatched me. If he gets sick or dies—"

She slammed her palm against the dash. *"Shut the fuck up."*

In that instant, she was as transparent as a piece of glass. Every line on her face told a different chapter from the same story—the pressure she was under, the worry, the fear, how far outside her comfort zone running a cartel had left her.

She was like a guitar, and all I had to do was pluck the right strings to get what I wanted.

I continued. "If he dies, then I don't really give a damn about anything else. You can do what you want to with that gun of mine."

She balled her fists, face mottled red with anger. She swore, banged the dash again.

"Fine, I'll get the kid his medicine."

I didn't react, hoping I'd made the right call. A moment passed, and she made her last mistake.

"He's here. The boy." She rubbed her eyes, looking ten years older all of a sudden. "You take care of Frank, and we'll get the kid his damn medicine."

- CHAPTER FORTY-ONE -

Mice and men. Their best-laid plans.

I realized what a colossal mistake I'd made as soon as we stepped inside.

Pax Larson-Ibarra lay dead on the floor, shot twice in the chest.

The air smelled like spent gunpowder. Urine darkened the crotch of his khakis, the stain spreading even as Quinn and I stood in the doorway.

He'd been killed seconds before.

No time to ponder why I hadn't heard a shot.

Noise from the rear of the house, footsteps, a body thumping into a piece of furniture.

I pulled the Beretta from my waistband, flicked off the safety—

Bam.

A bullet slammed into the wall a few feet away, plaster dust raining down on us.

I yanked Quinn to the floor.

Another blast and a window shattered.

Quinn huddled on her knees, shaking.

I dragged her toward the sitting room as a third round plowed into the woodwork over our heads.

We tumbled behind the sofa. The door to Frank's office was across the room.

"Is there another way out?" I asked.

She nodded. "Through the office. Leads to the kitchen."

I pulled her into Frank's room. Once there, we pressed our backs against the wall, breathing heavily.

The office was empty, dimly lit by a lamp on the desk.

"Where's Miguel?" I whispered.

"We had a deal. Frank's still alive."

"That was before your husband went off the rails and killed his partner. I need to make sure Miguel is safe before anything else happens."

Footsteps behind us in the room we'd just left, followed by silence.

I strained to hear, but there was no sound except the pounding of my own heart. After a moment, I looked at Quinn and pointed to the exit at the other end of the office.

She nodded. Together we crept in that direction.

That's when Frank appeared, stepping out of the shadows in front of us.

I wondered how he had managed to move from the room behind us to the other side of the house so quickly and silently.

He held the tiny semiauto in one hand, the other hand pressed against a wound in his side, blood seeping from between his fingers.

He spoke to Quinn. "Did you see him? He's in the house somewhere."

New info. There was someone else on the premises, not just Pax and Frank.

She didn't respond.

I glanced behind me, saw nothing. I prioritized the immediate threat, focusing all my attention on Frank.

He seemed to notice me for the first time. "What's he doing here?"

Quinn looked at me, her eyes wide, a weasel caught in the headlights.

I aimed the Beretta at Frank. "Put your gun down."

He wiped his mouth with his free hand, blood smearing across his chin. The weapon remained in his grasp.

Quinn finally spoke, her words directed at me. "Kill him."

Frank's mouth dropped open. He lowered the gun slightly, taken aback. "That's what this is about?"

"Do it," she said. "Shoot him."

"Drop your weapon." I eased closer.

"You bitch." He stared at his wife. "You money-grubbing tramp."

"Shoot him." Quinn jabbed a finger at the man she'd once promised to love and honor.

I didn't fire. My only goal at the moment was to find Miguel. Plus, I wasn't planning on killing anybody today other than her.

I took another step toward Frank, hoping to get close enough to disarm him. "Let's all be calm. Where's the bo—"

Thppt.

A rush of air over my shoulder and a spray of blood from Frank Vega's head. The top of his skull blew apart.

I whirled around, aiming the Beretta at—

Javier.

Standing in the doorway, a pistol in one hand. A pistol equipped with a silencer.

He said, "Put the gun down, amigo."

"What the hell are you doing?"

"Something I should have done a long time ago."

"Where did you get that?" I stared at the silencer.

"I just wanted to make my babies stop crying," he said. "I couldn't take it any longer."

Everything came back to me in a rush. El Corazón Roto, just after Sandoval had been killed, Javier knocking back Jack Daniel's even though it was barely noon. Javier starting to drink heavily after the restaurant guy was killed. Javier drunker than I've ever seen him after the Pecky Ruibal massacre.

Every time there was a killing, he got his whiskey on.

"You're the shooter?" I said.

Javier pointed to Frank Vega's corpse. "He told me that the cartel was coming to Dallas, the same people who killed my family."

"And he offered you a chance for vengeance," I said, finally understanding.

Javier nodded. "Take down the drug smugglers. He never said he was part of them."

Frank Vega may not have been street-smart, but he understood human nature.

Choosing a mournful father as his tool to take over the cartel's operation was a brilliant tactical move. Javier had a perfect motive, and he lived in a constant state of anger. He was like a cocked gun. He just needed pointing in the right direction.

"He lied to everybody," Quinn said.

I turned away from Javier.

Quinn had picked up her husband's pistol. "Put your weapons down, both of you."

I didn't move.

Javier stared at her. "What's going on?"

"Quinn fancies herself the brains of the operation," I said. "The narco godmother."

"What?" He frowned. "I don't understand."

She sneered at us. "Is it so hard to believe? A woman in charge of things."

"You got what you wanted," I said. "Your husband's dead. Now give me Miguel."

"She has the boy?" Javier lowered his gun, face aghast.

Quinn seized the opportunity. She fired, the bullet striking Javier in the shoulder.

He staggered backward, the gun staying in his grasp.

Quinn didn't seem to notice that he still had his weapon. She aimed at me. "You're next if you don't drop it."

"I want Miguel." I held on to the Beretta, the muzzle pointed to the floor.

She was about six feet away. I was an easy target, even for an untrained shooter. But so was she.

Her eyes narrowed as a vein twitched in her forehead.

From the front of the house came the sound of footsteps and voices in Spanish. The cavalry, such as it was, had arrived. Reinforcements, the people Frank had referenced in his phone call. Maybe members of the same gang as the two thugs at Rudy's earlier.

Either way, their arrival wasn't a good development for anybody.

Their connection had been through Pax, who lay dead on the floor of the entryway.

Quinn looked like she was going to call out to them.

I held my finger to my lips, hoping she'd understand that with Pax dead, whoever those gangbangers were, they would see themselves as free agents.

She took a step back, clearly terrified.

I stuck the Beretta in my waistband, moved closer to her, my hands up.

She didn't try to stop me.

When we were only a few inches apart, I whispered in her ear: "We need to get out of here. They're not your allies."

She was shaking, teeth chattering.

"Do you have more guns?" I asked. "Anything to help defend us."

She nodded. "The room above the garage. Locked in a safe."

I took a stab in the dark. "That's where the boy is, right?"

She hesitated. Then she nodded.

I tried to keep my face blank, to hide the elation I felt. I pointed to the door leading to the kitchen. "We'll go out the back."

When she looked that way, I twisted the gun from her hand while sliding my free arm around her neck, jamming her throat into the crook of my elbow.

She reacted as I suspected, not like someone trained for a street fight. She didn't jab a thumb in my eye or reach for my groin. Instead, she grabbed at my arm, trying to free herself.

With her gun still in my hand, I pressed the back of her head into my arm and squeezed. After a few moments, she stopped struggling.

Shouting in Spanish from the front of the house. Not much time left.

Javier stared at me from across the room, eyes wide.

I kept the pressure applied, sweat trickling down the small of my back.

A few seconds later, her body went slack.

Javier watched me ease her to the floor next to the corpse of her husband.

"Let's go." I pointed to the door leading to the kitchen.

He shook his head. "Get the boy. I'll slow them down."

- CHAPTER FORTY-TWO -

I dashed from Frank Vega's office and into the kitchen.

The room was all granite and stainless steel, copper pots hanging over a restaurant-grade stove.

French doors opened onto a patio, the garage visible about fifty feet away.

From the front of the house, people yelling.

I flung open the back door and headed toward the garage.

Gunfire behind me, Javier trying to slow them down.

The stairway to the second floor was on the outside of the structure. Exposed, vulnerable to whoever might exit the house and look toward the rear of the property.

That didn't matter.

I sprinted up the steps.

The door at the top was flimsy, glass paneled, secured by a single lock, not even a dead bolt.

Amateur hour here at Cartel HQ. Frank and Quinn Vega had been stooges all along, a means to an end. Run interference on controlling Texas.

Inside, I could see Miguel across the room, hands bound behind his back, a gag in his mouth. I reared back a leg, kicked right above the lock.

The door sprang open.

I ran inside, dropped Quinn's gun on the floor, pulled off the gag. "Are you OK?"

He nodded.

The room was one big open area, a kitchenette along the far wall by an open door leading to a bathroom.

I flung open drawers until I found a paring knife. Then I cut the plastic ties around his wrists and ankles. He threw his arms around me and began to cry. I hugged him for a moment, trying to keep my emotions under control. Then I pushed him away. We needed to leave the Vega property as soon as possible.

Quinn's Mercedes was by the front. I still had the key, but I didn't want to risk getting that close to the house.

"We have to get out of here," I said. *"Pronto."*

Miguel's face was pale, his breathing shallow and rapid.

"We'll find a back way out." I stood. "We just have to be quick going down the steps."

He nodded, followed me to the door.

The hood was about halfway up the stairs. He had teardrop tattoos under both eyes and a pistol in his hand.

I pulled the Beretta from my waistband. I aimed at the same time as he began to raise his weapon. He was below me, so his gun had farther to travel.

I fired, the bullet striking him in the lower abdomen.

He didn't fall, however, grasping the railing with one hand, the other slowly bringing the gun up.

I fired twice more, both rounds hitting him in the chest.

He tumbled down the steps, leaving a trail of blood as he went.

At the base of the stairs, I jumped over his body, motioning for Miguel to do the same.

At the front of the house, I could see a Chevy Impala with low-profile tires and chrome wheels parked behind Quinn's Mercedes.

Figure there had been four people in the Chevy, and one was now dead.

What about the other three?

There was no movement from the house.

Miguel tugged on my arm. *"Está Javier aquí?"*

I didn't reply. Miguel looked at the house, his eyes wide.

"Dónde está Javier?" he said.

I put a hand on his shoulder.

"No, no, no." He shook his head.

"Él no está aquí," I said. "Not any longer, anyway."

The boy stared at me, tears in his eyes.

I pointed to the gate by the garage, which led to the street. *"Vámonos."*

• • •

We walked north on Fisher Road.

Javier's pickup was parked in an alley on the other side, out of view of the front entrance to the Vega property. Miguel craned his neck to keep the truck in sight as we passed it.

We'd made it about sixty yards when the first police car blew by, lights and sirens blaring.

That much gunfire in a quiet, upscale neighborhood meant the area was going to be crawling with police.

I had an arm on Miguel's shoulder, trying to project an image of normalcy, just two fellows out for an afternoon stroll.

Once the squad car passed us, I pulled the Beretta from my waistband and ejected the magazine, thumbing bullets into the drainage ditch on the side of the road as we walked. When the mag was empty, I wiped it down with my T-shirt and tossed it across the street into a thicket of honeysuckle.

Miguel looked up at me. *"A dónde vamos?"*

"I don't know where we're going." I removed the slide from the frame. "We'll figure it out as we go. *Está bien?"*

He nodded.

I wiped down both sections of the gun, dropping the slide into a puddle of water on our side of the street, tossing the frame into a culvert on the other.

Two more squad cars sped by.

"I'm sorry we came back to Dallas," I said.

He didn't reply, and we kept walking.

CHAPTER FORTY-THREE -

We continued on for about thirty minutes, until we got to Mockingbird Lane, the first major thoroughfare north of the Vega residence.

Neither of us spoke.

Looking back, I suppose I was in a state of shock. Javier had been the killer all along, manipulated by Frank Vega. And I had missed it.

I wondered what would have happened if I hadn't encountered him all those months ago, preparing to end his own life. Would he have killed himself, and none of this would have occurred? Would his death have derailed the plans of Frank and Quinn Vega?

Shoulda, coulda, woulda. The seductive call of hindsight.

I pushed those thoughts from my mind. The past was the past. Nothing ever remained for any of us but the future, for good or bad.

One thing was certain: if I'd never met Javier, I wouldn't have met Miguel. For this I was grateful.

I still had my wallet, so I bought a burner at CVS and called Aloysius Throckmorton. After talking to him, I strolled over to the 7-Eleven and purchased a one-gallon plastic gas can and package of Styrofoam cups. Outside, I filled the gas can with diesel fuel.

Miguel and I sat on a curb. While we waited, I tore a dozen or so cups into tiny pieces, adding them to the diesel fuel. The petroleum product melted the Styrofoam, forming a flammable jelly.

Homemade napalm.

Twenty minutes later, I was sitting in the front seat of Throckmorton's Suburban. Miguel sat in the rear, the gas can in the cargo area.

"What have you fellows been up to since we had breakfast?" Throckmorton said.

"A little of this, a little of that." I buckled the seat belt.

"There's a multiple homicide south of here on Fisher Road. You know anything about that?"

I didn't respond.

"Frank Vega's place, sounds like." He shifted in his seat.

"What we talked about before. It's over." I paused. "For the moment."

He stared out the window but didn't speak.

"Can you give us a ride?" I asked.

"Do I look like one o' them U-bear drivers?" He smiled.

I smiled back. A small measure of the tension from the last few weeks began to dissipate. We weren't safe yet, not by a long shot, but all the immediate threats had been eliminated.

All but one.

"Bus station?" he asked.

"I need to make a stop first."

• • •

Most gun shops are built to be secure, burglar bars on the windows, concrete pillars in front of the doors, that sort of thing.

Stodghill's place was no different. From past visits, I knew he'd even installed reinforced, fireproof walls between his operation and the other two businesses, the modeling studio and the print shop. The walls

248

went all the way to the ceiling, which was reinforced and fireproof as well, just in case someone tried to access his area from the crawl space or the roof.

In effect, his shop was one large fireproof safe, designed to keep disaster out.

The reverse was true as well.

I asked Throckmorton to stop at the end of the block, told him I could walk the rest of the way. I had already told him that Stodghill had something of mine that was incriminating. I gave him no details, and he didn't ask for any.

Miguel reached for the door handle, but I motioned for him to stay put.

"I never did like that Stodghill guy," Throckmorton said. "Sold anything to anybody."

I nodded in agreement.

Throckmorton pointed to the back. "What's with the gas can?"

I shrugged.

Neither of us spoke for a few moments.

"How you planning on getting in?" he asked.

"Ring the bell? See what happens."

Not the best plan but the only one I had at the moment.

"You really think that's going to work?" He pulled away from the curb.

• • •

Miguel stayed in the Suburban, which was idling at the edge of the parking lot.

I stood to one side of the metal door, gas can in one hand, out of view of the camera.

Throckmorton pushed the buzzer and stood so the video system could see him, his badge gleaming in the afternoon sun.

The solenoid clicked, and I walked in behind Throckmorton.

Stodghill stood behind the counter. The place was empty otherwise. He smiled until he saw me. "What the hell?"

"Howdy," Throckmorton said. "You're under arrest."

"For what?"

"For being a shitass. We'll worry about the specifics later." He motioned for him to come out from behind the counter.

Stodghill did so reluctantly, staring at me as he walked.

Throckmorton said, "Put your hands on your head."

"What the hell is going on?"

Throckmorton grabbed his arm and threw him facedown on one of the counters. He searched him, removing three pistols: one in his waistband, another in a shoulder holster, a third affixed to his ankle.

He then cuffed the man and placed him on the floor, legs spread.

"You need me, I'll be outside." He left.

Stodghill stared at me, lips curled into a sneer.

After the door shut, I said, "Is anyone else here?"

He didn't reply for a moment. Then he shook his head.

I searched anyway, found no one else.

The area immediately behind the front was a storeroom full of boxed-up weapons, mostly long guns marked PRIVATE SALES, the first of the stock for the new venture at the Aztec Bazaar.

There were also crates of ammunition and several gun safes. Behind that was a small apartment—a single bedroom, a sitting area, and a kitchen. The bed was neatly made and the kitchen sparkling clean.

A sad scene, this man's life. Lonely, living amid weapons of destruction, many of which were destined for use by a drug cartel.

I wondered how he had gotten to this point in his existence. Did people think my life was sad as well? I didn't spend much time pondering any of that.

Back in the front, I dribbled about half the homemade napalm over a shelf full of ammunition. The ammo was beneath a rack of long guns.

Stodghill watched. "What are you doing?"

After thinking about it for a moment, I stepped back into the storeroom and emptied the gas can over the stack of guns destined for private sales.

I went back to the front.

The store also sold reloading supplies, various powders and primers and bullets used to make your own ammunition.

I opened a can of powder and ran a trail from the napalm covering the ammunition to a spot by the front door.

"What the hell do you want, Arlo?"

I didn't say anything, thinking that should have been pretty obvious. I rummaged around in a drawer by the cash register until I found a book of matches.

"For God's sake, have you lost your mind?" Stodghill struggled against the cuffs.

I stood by the front door, matches in hand. "Where's my Glock?"

His eyes went wide.

I tore a match from the book.

"You wouldn't." He paused. "You can't."

"Yeah, I would."

"Bullshit. You're not a murderer."

I lit the match.

"The middle safe." He rattled off the combination. "That's where your gun is."

I blew out the match and left him there. In the back, I opened the safe.

The manila envelope was on a shelf in the middle, next to several pistol boxes. I looked inside, saw my Glock and the paperwork. I tucked the envelope under my arm and went back to the front.

"Let me go," he said. "You have what you came for."

I stared at his face for a long moment, giving him the cop glare.

He stared back, trying to be tough. After a few seconds, he looked away and began to hyperventilate.

"Give me the combos to the other safes."

He shook his head, eyes fearful.

I lit a match.

"Please," he said. "You got what you came for."

I held out the match.

The flame burned closer to my fingers.

"Ow," I said. "That's getting hot."

"All right, all right." He sighed.

I blew out the match, and he gave me the information. I entered the storeroom and opened the other safes, leaving their contents exposed.

Back in the front room, I pulled the matches from my pocket.

"What do you want now?" he asked. "What else is there?"

"Nothing." I paused. "Everyone but you is dead."

He frowned. "What do you mean?"

"Frank and Quinn. Pax. Javier."

His face turned white. "Are you going to kill me?"

"Maybe. That's up to you." I pulled him to his feet. "If you tell anybody about me or Throckmorton, you're a dead man. I will hunt you down to the ends of the earth."

He realized what was about to happen. "Please don't do this. The store, it's all I have."

I shoved him out the door. Then I lit a match.

• • •

Throckmorton took me to a bridge over White Rock Lake where I stripped the Glock and threw the pieces as far as possible in opposite directions. Then he dropped us off at the bus station downtown, the same place where Javier and I had found Miguel.

"Where you headed?" he asked.

"You really want to know?"

He shook his head and looked at Miguel. "You take care of yourself, OK, partner?"

The boy nodded.

"You too, Arlo. Be safe."

I thanked him for all he had done, and then Miguel and I entered the station.

The next bus going anywhere north was at 6:30 p.m., a little over an hour from now, heading for Tulsa with stops in Ardmore and Oklahoma City.

I bought two tickets, and we went next door to McDonald's.

After we'd eaten, we sat in the terminal and waited for our bus to be called.

A few minutes later, Miguel looked at me. "Do you think Javier is still alive?"

I didn't speak, unsure how to answer. Finally, I shook my head.

He nodded but didn't speak.

"He stayed behind so we could get away," I said.

Miguel slipped his hand into mine.

"Javier was a good man," I said.

The boy leaned against my shoulder. A moment later, he was asleep.

ACKNOWLEDGMENTS

Creating a work of fiction is a group experience. The raw material may have been mine, but the end result is a communal effort, thanks to a dedicated group of professionals who are as much responsible for what you hold in your hand as the author is. To that end, I would like to thank everybody at Thomas & Mercer: Dennelle Catlett, David Downing, Gracie Doyle, Megha Parekh, and Sarah Shaw. Also, many thanks to Richard Abate for helping make this book possible at the outset.

For their help with the manuscript, I would like to offer my gratitude to Jan Blankenship, Victoria Calder, Paul Coggins, Peggy Fleming, Alison Hunsicker, Fanchon Henneberger, Brooke Malouf, Clif Nixon, David Norman, Glenna Whitley, and Max Wright.

ABOUT THE AUTHOR

Photo © 2013 Nick McWhirter

Harry Hunsicker is the former executive vice president of the Mystery Writers of America and the author of seven crime thrillers, including *The Devil's Country*, the first Arlo Baines novel, and the Jon Cantrell and Lee Henry Oswald series. His work has been short-listed for both the Shamus and Thriller Awards. Hunsicker's story "West of Nowhere," originally published in *Ellery Queen Mystery Magazine*, was selected for inclusion in the anthology *The Best American Mystery Stories 2011*. For more about Harry, visit him at www.harryhunsicker.com.

ABOUT THE AUTHOR